THE HEARTWOOD SEA

A HEARTWOOD SISTERS NOVEL (CARTER'S COVE BOOK 1)

ELANA JOHNSON

ISBN-13:

1

Alissa Heartwood knew it was time to get up before her alarm even went off. Waking before dawn for the past decade could do that to a person. She had two of the most important jobs for The Heartwood Inn, the family-run hotel, resort, and restaurant on the popular island of Carter's Cove, and they both started in the middle of the night.

One of the very last family-run establishments, the way the big corporations with their big checks and big pens had been coming in. Literally, great big checks that took three people to hold them while cameras clicked.

But Alissa's family had stayed the course, and their "inn" was more of a luxury resort these days, with that downhome family feel people craved, even if they didn't know it.

Alissa's job was to bring in the catch-of-the-day on her

trusty shrimp boat, and everyone knew the best time to get fish was before the sun rose. She didn't mind, as she loved the calmness of the Atlantic Ocean as it got painted with the first rays of glorious, golden sunlight each day.

Well, at least each day in the height of the summer season, which it currently was.

After that, Alissa slicked back her hair into a tight bun and started on the pastries for the day. She'd been professionally trained for four long years of pastry school, and people could come into Heartwood just for their bakery.

Her creations.

Handmade, every morning.

The best part of Alissa's job was that she finished by one o'clock, though most people didn't know that was the end of a ten-hour work day.

Alissa knew it, and her back knew it, and the last of the summer cold she'd been fighting for weeks knew it. Still, she got dressed, not bothering to shower, and whistled for Dodger and Pirate to join her.

She lived in her grandparent's old house, as only her grandmother remained alive now, and she'd moved in with Alissa's parents when they'd officially retired from the Heartwood empire. Alissa's oldest sister, Olympia, ran things now, and Alissa took a moment in the darkness to appreciate everything she had.

Sure, maybe she was lonely at night. Even in the afternoons, boredom found her. She needed a summer boyfriend, but she'd had one of those, thank you very much, and he'd left the island with most of her heart.

She'd tried dating a bit over the winter, but it was a half-hearted attempt, and she knew it. *Half-hearted.* She chuckled at her own lame joke, because it wasn't funny what Calvin had done with her heart, and headed toward the dock across the sand.

Very few houses sat along the beach, as the hurricane season in South Carolina was no joke. But somehow, the Heartwood cottage where her grandparents had raised four daughters and a son had weathered all the storms over the years.

Alissa boarded *Big Blue*, patting the side of the boat like she did every morning. "Morning, Blue," she said to the vessel as if it could respond. "Lots of shrimp today, okay? It's Monday, and we get a lot of families in on Mondays."

Especially if they came before seven, as kids ate free with a paying adult on Mondays. After that, cocktail hour began, and Redfin, the restaurant another of Alissa's sisters managed, became crowded with adults holding delicate flutes of champagne, women wearing slinky dresses and men decked out in polos.

"Maybe I should go to cocktail hour tonight," she said to Dodger, who'd just put his paws up on the doorknob, as if the German shepherd couldn't wait to get inside the steering room. But the dog hated it in there. He'd probably left a ball in the corner somewhere. Alissa wouldn't put it past him; the dog was as smart as they come.

Alissa unlocked the door and let Dodger in. Pirate, a much smaller basset hound, followed. Alissa moved around all the dials and switches with the ease of a seasoned pro. Of course, she *was* a seasoned pro, as she'd been heading out at three a.m. on this boat since she was five years old.

A pang of missing for her grandfather hit her, and she touched two fingers to her lips and said, "Love you, Grandpa," before starting the engine. *Big Blue* groaned, but she came to life, and Alissa's face burst into a smile. "Good girl."

She backed out of the dock, flipped on her lights, and sent up a quick plea for a lot of shrimp. She didn't want to deal with Gwen's attitude about having to buy from the bigger commercial boats if Alissa couldn't bring in enough shrimp.

Of course, it happened. She was one boat, while the commercial fisheries had whole teams of people, boats, and fishing spots. She just had the traps and lines she'd been setting for years now, though it did help that she didn't have to go out as far as they did, and they couldn't come into her waters and poach from her.

Captaining the boat brought Alissa a slip of happiness, but she still knew *Big Blue* wouldn't be there to keep her warm at night, ask her about her day, or bring her roses.

Fine, she didn't really want roses.

Or maybe she did.

At this point, she wasn't sure. All she knew was that there had to be more to life than waking up in the middle of the night, emptying lobster traps, and then making panna cotta and blueberry croissants.

Hours later, she still hadn't worked out the meaning of life, but she felt confident she'd have enough shrimp to satisfy Gwen for the day.

The sun had come up already, and Alissa knew from experience that it was going to be a scorcher of a day. She wiped sweat from her forehead and replaced her disgusting shrimp boat captain hat before texting Gwen to send down her kitchen hands to get all the fish. Long ago, the water had gone almost to the restaurant, and the chutes in the bottom of the boat could be used to get the fish into the kitchen.

But the shoreline had receded a lot over the past few decades, due to more building, more expansion on the island. More wealth. More people discovering the gem of Carter's Cove and booking their family vacations, honeymoons, weddings, anniversaries, and birthday celebrations on the island.

In the summer, the population doubled as tourists poured into town, and yet there always seemed to be enough hotels, enough swimming pools, and enough golf courses to keep everyone happy.

At least Alissa thought so. A new high-rise hotel had

started being built just a half a block from her family's land, where they had five homes of various sizes. Alissa didn't share her grandparents' place, but a couple of her sisters shared, with Olympia living full time in the hotel itself.

Theirs was probably the last bit of undeveloped land on the island, though Alissa knew there were wild spots over on the north side too.

Dodger barked as he hit the sand running, and Alissa shaded her eyes as she looked up. Gwen hadn't responded to her text, but she'd obviously gotten it, as several men walked toward them, big, black containers in their hands. Pirate waddled on the sand, and the simple sight of it made Alissa smile.

"Hey, guys," she said, flashing what she hoped was a bright smile at the guys. She thought she was a decent flirt, but none of the kitchen hands had ever asked her out.

That's because Gwen's the cute blonde, Alissa told herself, forcing herself not to turn around and walk backward in the sand. She wasn't a supermodel by any stretch of the imagination, but she liked her curves.

All the right curves in all the right places. At least that was what her mother had always said.

She entered the kitchen through the back door of the restaurant, her calves burning from the long march up the beach. Since she'd thought of blueberry croissants that morning, she hadn't been able to get them out of her head.

But they weren't on her weekly list for the menu, so she couldn't make them. Gwen would have a fit then, and Alissa didn't need the drama in her life. Or maybe she did. Maybe it would be nice to have some drama for a change.

No one bothered her in the pastry nook, and the temperature in the kitchen only increased as the next couple of hours passed. Alissa felt like she'd melt into a puddle of sweat, despite the fan that blew in the corner.

She paused in her work and stepped over to the sink, turning the water on as cold as it would go. Then she practically dunked her head under the stream, the relief to her steamed face instant and refreshing.

"Alissa," Olympia called, and she lifted her head out of the industrial-sized sink.

"Back here."

Her sister's heels clicked toward her, and it wasn't the only pair of footsteps. Alissa couldn't see who she'd brought with her, but it was definitely a man with broad shoulders in one of those annoying polos.

It wasn't even noon yet, and Alissa had no idea what her sister could possibly need from her.

"There you are," Olympia said, as if Alissa had been hard to find.

"Here I am." Her face dripped with water, and she didn't care—until the man stepped out from behind Olympia.

Though she had water droplets clinging to her eyelashes, Alissa could still make out the very handsome face of Shawn Newman.

She sucked in a breath.

The Shawn Newman from her childhood. Teenhood. Whatever.

She searched frantically for a towel, and of course, all such things seemed to have departed the area.

Shawn smiled, and oh, that wasn't fair. He still had that same chestnut hair, those same sparkling blue eyes that had always teased her, even right as he was about to kiss her. Today, he wore a pair of blue board shorts and that blasted polo in lavender, and dang if Alissa's heart didn't beat faster and faster....

It was definitely whole enough for him to break it.

Lavender. She almost scoffed. What kind of man wore lavender?

Shawn Newman, her mind whispered.

"I need you to show Mister Newman around," Olympia said, and alarms sounded through Alissa with the professional, clipped tone of her sister's voice.

"What?" she asked.

"You two were friends in high school, right?" Olympia practically looked down her nose at Alissa, but without those heels, they'd be eye-to-eye.

Friends. Another scoff-worthy word. "Yeah," Alissa said, dragging out the vowels at the end of the word. "Friends."

With benefits, but Shawn just stood there, his winning smile on his face. Alissa wished she wasn't dripping wet and boiling hot. She probably looked like a homeless dog who'd just fallen into pond scum.

"He's back in town for a couple of weeks, and he'll be staying with us," Olympia said. "I've sent you a text with the details of what he needs."

"Why—?"

"Thanks, Liss." Olympia put her fake business smile on her face and turned to Shawn. "She's all yours."

Oh, no she wasn't, and Alissa bristled at the words. At the question her sister had silenced.

Why me?

Alissa didn't deal with high-profile guests. Any of the other sisters would've been a better choice. And she certainly didn't have time for Shawn Newman, his brilliant smile, or the jittery feeling in her stomach.

Shawn Newman drank in the sight of Alissa Heartwood as she watched her sister march away. She wiped one hand down her face, effectively stopping the water from dripping off her chin.

He had no idea what to say, and his cheeks were starting to hurt from the incessant smiling. He consciously removed the grin from his face and hooked his thumb over his shoulder.

"She hasn't changed."

"Yeah, well, neither have you." Alissa pushed past him and took a few strides over to a stainless steel counter, where she picked up a towel and buried her face in it.

Shawn twisted toward her, his pulse rapid-firing in the vein in his neck. He hadn't expected a warm welcome, by any stretch of the imagination. But the cold shoulder?

He knew from experience that Lissa could give the

iciest of looks—sometimes just a few seconds before she kissed him.

Licking his lips like that might actually happen, Shawn then swallowed. After all, he hadn't returned to Carter's Cove for a relaxing beach vacation. Or a new girlfriend. Oh, he had one of those back in Miami.

Well, sort of. Lauren would definitely say they were dating, as would Lauren's father—the man who'd sent Shawn here to get the Heartwood land.

"What do you want, Shawn?" Lissa asked, turning and cocking her hip.

He was grateful he'd left the folder of contracts up in his hotel room. Everything he'd told Olympia Heartwood was true. He was in town for a couple of weeks. He was staying at the hotel.

But what she didn't know—what no one knew—was that he was there to *buy* the hotel. And as much of the surrounding land as he could. All the way to the beach.

"Nothing," he said.

"Then why did my sister say she'd text me the details of what you need?" Her aquamarine eyes shot lasers at him, and dang if Shawn didn't want to get sliced right in half by her.

He knew exactly what that felt like, even though they'd broken up before they'd graduated. Before she went off to pastry school, and he went to the University of Miami.

He'd been down in Florida ever since, only coming

back to the island where he'd grown up periodically to celebrate anniversaries, birthdays, or the holidays with his family.

"Are you deaf?" Lissa asked, and Shawn blinked.

"Not deaf," he said. "Sorry, it was just a long flight this morning."

"A long flight from Miami?" She scoffed and dunked her hands in a huge bowl of dough. "It's less than two hours, Shawn."

He shook his head. Of course he'd known running into Alissa Heartwood was a possibility. But he also knew Olympia managed the family business now, and he'd hoped he'd only have to deal with the oldest Heartwood.

But Olympia had barely given him the time of day, almost like she knew exactly why he'd come and booked a room without a check-out date. And now she'd passed him off to Alissa.

"I want a tour of the place," he said, clearing his throat and trying to center his thoughts. "I want to see everything the public does, and everything they don't."

Her eyes narrowed, but she didn't stop pulling the bread from the bowl. She picked up a knife that looked incredibly sharp, and Shawn fell back a step. She cocked her right eyebrow, as if she knew exactly why he'd moved.

"Why?"

"I've missed this place." He put his closer smile on his face, but Lissa didn't even flinch.

"You're still not a great liar," she said, sliding that knife through the dough easily, separating it into chunks she put on a scale before tossing them onto a tray.

"What time are you done?" Shawn asked.

"None of your business."

A sigh moved through his whole body, but he didn't let it out. "I'll catch you later then." He didn't wait for another cutting remark, though part of him wanted to. He left the kitchen, noticing that everything inside the old mansion on the beach had been redone.

This inn was breathtaking on the inside and out, and it would be a real shame for it to be anything but what it was. The sigh did come out then, and he went out the exit and leaned against the railing. The beach in front of him felt tranquil, with all the perfect grains of sand. The waves chatted with him, and he loved the sound of them.

Miami had plenty of beaches too. Lots of waves. But somehow, everything here was different. More tranquil. Slower.

"Kind of exactly what you want," he murmured to himself. He wasn't sure what he wanted anymore. He knew if he closed this deal, he'd get the promotion he'd been working for the past five years to get. He did love his life in Miami, inside the big apartment on the twentieth floor. The views there were great, and the night life in the city and on the beaches was something to behold.

But Shawn didn't usually leave the apartment after dark unless it was to check out a property he needed to see in action. A nightclub. A restaurant, a pub. Something like that. He was getting too old for such things, and this beach where he'd spent a lot of his childhood whispered to him that maybe it was time to settle down.

He turned away from the water, from his thoughts. To distract himself, he texted his brother, Bo. *Made it to town. Can I stay with you?*

I thought you had a room at your girlfriend's hotel.

1. *She's not my girlfriend. We broke up almost twenty years ago. B. I think staying here is a bad idea.*

Haha. Sure. You know where I live.

Without second-guessing himself, he went up to his room and collected his luggage and his dog. "Come on, Gentleman. We're going to see Uncle Bo." The golden retriever jumped down from the bed like he'd been waiting for Shawn to make this decision all along.

He did know where Bo lived, and he knew it was easy to get around the island in the summer. Taxis lined up outside of the hotels, and The Heartwood Inn was no different. His brother wasn't there, as he ran one of the transportation businesses on the island, and they literally worked twenty hours a day during tourist season.

Shawn had hated the tourist season growing up. His family owned a golf course, and his father made everyone work the course from an early age. Shawn was the middle child of five, and he'd picked up more golf balls than a human being should ever have to.

His oldest sister Jen ran the golf course now, and Shannon had left the island with her husband. She lived in Washington D.C. with her family, and Shawn's two younger brothers had stayed on the island, getting into tourism as well.

They had good lives, but only Shannon was married with kids. The rest of Shawn's siblings—and himself— were married to their jobs.

Shawn had never minded the long hours he worked. Not having any time to date was just fine with him, especially after Rhiannon had cut out his heart and left the state of Florida with it in her back pocket.

He'd started "dating" the boss's daughter, and he'd climbed quickly at work. And he just had one more step to take. He took a very big breath and re-centered his thoughts.

The Heartwood Inn. That was why he'd come.

He called them and asked for Alissa, and the receptionist said, "She's not here, sir. She leaves at one."

A smile formed on his face, and he said, "Thank you," before hanging up. A new plan formed in his mind, and he'd need a cup of coffee with a lot of cream and a bag of chocolate chip cookies before he saw Lissa again.

Oh, and maybe a prayer that she still liked her coffee with a lot of cream, dogs, and could eat chocolate chip cookies for every meal. She couldn't have changed that much, could she?

AN HOUR LATER, SHAWN FEARED THE CHOCOLATE CHIP cookies had melted completely. He felt like he'd melted into the sand, and he still hadn't seen the blonde he couldn't get out of his head. He knew her family owned all the property along this beach. Maybe she'd seen him and disappeared inside whichever house she was currently living in.

Gentleman had swam out into the water every time Shawn threw the ball, but even now the dog simply walked at his side, his tongue lolling out.

A different dog barked, and Shawn turned toward the sound at the same time Gentleman talked back. A moment later, the beast came bounding down the sand a ways, back toward a beach cottage that had to belong to someone in the Heartwood family. Shawn had walked by it three times already on his fake quest to find the perfect spot of sand to spend the afternoon.

"Dodger!" a woman called after him as Shawn chuckled and bent down to pat the German shepherd as he and Gentleman started a sniffing war.

He knew that voice, besides. It was Lissa, and Shawn couldn't believe his good luck in finally finding her. Of course, the heat burning into his bare shoulders testified that maybe he wasn't as lucky as he thought. He had been wandering for an hour, after all.

He straightened as another dog approached, this one

just as friendly as Dodger, but definitely smaller. He circled Shawn and Gentleman like he was herding them, and Dodger turned back the way he'd come as if to lead them all home. Unwilling to let the pups down, Shawn said, "Come on, Gentleman," and went with the dogs.

Cresting a sandy hill, he caught sight of Lissa looking the wrong way down the beach. "Dodger!" she called now, twisting toward him. She saw them, turning fully toward him now. "Sorry," she said, coming forward. "They're a little—" She paused and muted, and she'd obviously realized who he was.

Her eyes hid behind a dark pair of sunglasses, but Shawn could still feel her gaze moving down to his bare feet and back to his face. "What are you doing here?"

"You've asked me that once already," he said, lifting the white bakery bag that held her messy cookies. "I'm just spending an afternoon on the beach with my dog and a snack." He wasn't sure if she looked at the bag or not. "I guess your dogs like chocolate chip cookies as much as you do."

She harrumphed and turned around. "Come on, guys," she said, and the dogs trotted over to her as she moved toward that cottage.

Dodger turned back and barked, and Lissa said, "No, they're not coming." She could certainly glare through those shades, though she did look at Gentleman a little too long. So she definitely still loved dogs. Obviously, as she had two of them.

Shawn really wanted to go with her, and it had nothing to do with his job. "Maybe we could come in for a sec," he said, walking toward her. "Gentleman needs a drink." She opened her mouth to say something, but it closed as he sidled up to her and continued, all three dogs coming with him now.

Satisfaction dove through him, but his heart pulsed irregularly when Lissa didn't catch up to them. He finally turned back to find her gazing out at the ocean, the indecision streaming from her in waves.

She turned and somehow their eyes met despite her sunglasses. "Fine," she said, finally moving toward him. "But you have to put on a shirt." Her glare sliced right through him as she approached and passed him, and wow, Shawn had been missing so much in his life because she wasn't in it.

3

Alissa marched through the sand though she wanted to stroll. Her calf muscles screamed at her to slow down already, but she kept up the pace. Shawn huffed and puffed beside her, and he had pulled a gray T-shirt over his head, thank goodness. She couldn't be near him with all that golden skin showing. All those muscles.

She almost shivered though the temperature and humidity today were enough to melt steel. Or so it seemed.

A blast of air-conditioned air hit her as she went through the front door. She'd just spent an hour on the beach with the dogs as they splashed in the surf. They went straight for their water bowls and made a ruckus as they started slurping.

Behind her, Shawn sighed in relief and closed the door behind him. "Was this your grandparents' place?"

"Yes," she said curtly as she turned on the water. She got out two glasses and put ice in them, eyeing Shawn as he looked around her cottage. His reappearance in her life wasn't exactly unwelcome, but she didn't know what to make of it. He hadn't been home for a while, and even when he came to visit his parents, he never stayed long. Never looked her up. They hadn't spoken in years and years.

"It's nice," he finally said, looking at her.

"You're fried," she said, filling the glasses. She set one on the counter for him and drank from the other. Maybe if she filled her stomach with ice water, she'd stop thinking heated things about the man in front of her.

Problem was, she remembered everything about him. The way his hand fit in hers. The way he'd chuckle softly against her neck when they laid together in the bed of a truck he'd parked on the north beach, where not many tourists went. The way his mouth felt against hers. The taste of him.

She jerked to attention as he reached for the glass of water. Alissa pushed off the counter and went to get the dog bowls. She washed them out and refilled them before turning to him. "Do you have aloe vera at the hotel? You're going to need it." It so wasn't fair of him to bring a beautiful golden retriever with him.

"I'm not at the hotel anymore," he said.

"Yeah, we don't allow dogs." She cocked her head and folded her arms, trying to figure him out.

"Olympia said she'd make an exception."

"I bet she regretted that once she figured out why you're here."

He skated his eyes past her, and he was so much a salesman.

"You want to buy Heartwood," she said. "You should know it's not for sale."

"I know that."

She leaned her hip into the counter. "Is that your high-rise going up down the block?"

"Not mine specifically," he said, though the hotel did belong to the Tremmel Group.

"Your company, then."

"I don't own a company."

Alissa was so done with this conversation. "You should go. Get some aloe vera for your shoulders and face." She walked out of the kitchen and into the living room, intending to show him the door.

"Olympia told me the hotel and land wasn't for sale," Shawn said, following her.

"Then why are you still here?" Alissa really needed him to answer the question. "Why come at all? You could've had her tell you we weren't selling on the phone." He could've stayed in Miami, with his surely skinny, tan girlfriend, his corner office, and his luxury apartment. Oh, and that dog Alissa really wanted.

"I needed a vacation," he said. "And this deal just happened to coincide with that." He joined her near the front door, and there wasn't enough space for the both of them.

"There's no deal," she said.

"I can see that," he said, his bright blue eyes almost causing intoxication when she looked into them for longer than a few seconds. "Maybe you'll keep the cookies anyway? And maybe I'll see you around the island. I'll be here for a few weeks." His hand brushed hers, and every muscle in Alissa's body seized. "Gentleman would love to play with Dodger and Pirate."

Pure heat wove through her, making her mind soft. She had no idea what he'd just said, and his fingers weren't even touching hers anymore.

"Do they still do the hot air balloon festival on the Fourth?" he asked.

She nodded.

"And the motorcycle parade?"

"Of course," she said, her voice far too choked for her liking. Shawn would be able to hear it. He had to know how good-looking he was. How charming. How boring her life was and how un-boring he could make it.

She'd been dreading all the island summer activities, as she hated all the noise, the crowds, and the entertainment she had to face alone. But with him at her side....

He's not at your side, she told herself. *He wants to buy everything your family has worked for and turn it into a golf course.*

Olympia had given her details once they were both

free from Shawn. "However you got rid of him, keep it up," her sister had said. "We're not selling, no matter the price."

Alissa had agreed, of course. She loved the inn, the restaurant, the bakery, all of it. The Heartwood's did own a lot of prime real estate, and Shawn wasn't the first developer that had come with a folder and a number. He likely wouldn't be the last.

Didn't mean the Heartwoods were interested in selling.

"Okay, well, never mind," he said, snapping Alissa back to the conversation at hand.

"I'm sorry," she said as he walked out the front door. "What?"

Shawn turned back to her, somewhat of a glare on his face. "I asked you if you wanted to ride in the parade with me. You can say no. You don't have to ignore me." He shook his head. "Never mind. I'll find a bike and ride myself." He went down the steps quickly, and Alissa didn't have time to process what he'd said.

He'd asked her to ride with him in the motorcycle parade?

As he left, Alissa couldn't stop the memories from marching through her mind. Their first date had been at the motorcycle parade, the summer between their junior and senior years. Pure excitement had flowed through her as she perched on the back of a sexy, black motorcycle, Shawn's broad shoulders in front of her. She'd wrapped her arms around him, leaned when he leaned, and kissed him late, late that night as fireworks exploded into the sky.

So maybe she shouldn't have kissed him on the first date. But they'd grown up on the island together, and she'd known him well. He wasn't a player, and he never pressured her to do more than she wanted to.

Their relationship had lasted eight months, until Marcy Myers had sent him a Val-o-gram, stolen his attention, and he'd broken up with Alissa.

Did he even remember that? Did he care?

"Why would he ask me to ride in the parade with him?" Wonder filled Alissa, but not nearly as much as the frustration and confusion that kept her air-conditioning the entire beach in front of the cottage.

She finally got herself together enough to close the door, but she couldn't do much more than move to the couch and collapse onto it. Dodger and Pirate both jumped onto the sofa beside her, their tongues still hanging out of their mouths.

"Why'd you have to go round him up?" she asked Dodger. "He wasn't someone to bring home." Even if Alissa was imagining what it would be like to have him for her boyfriend again, all these years later.

"You're just lonely," she told herself as she turned on the TV. She'd take a nap, and order dinner when she woke up, and tomorrow would be just like today—minus the troubling reappearance of Shawn Newman in her life.

THE NEXT DAY STARTED JUST AS HER DAYS HAD FOR MONTHS and years. Fishing. Baking. Dealing with Gwen's wrath over the catch. Fielding family texts that came in too fast. Avoiding Olympia when she came into the kitchen with the hotel's housekeeping manager. They both seemed to have a storm raging around them, and Alissa didn't need any more drama in her life.

"Oh, good, you're still here."

"I'm still here," she said, looking at Harriett, the bakery manager. Alissa wiped the counter where she'd been working. No one touched her baking station while she was gone, other than to pull out the extra pans of brownies and cheesecakes she'd made and bake them off.

"Someone just came in and wants to order fifteen dozen doughnuts for a party tonight. I told him I'd ask and see if we could handle that." Harriett wore a sympathetic expression on her face. "It's fine if we can't. We have a twenty-four-hour policy on big orders."

Alissa sighed. Fifteen dozen doughnuts was a lot of doughnuts. A few hours worth of work. "I can do it."

"Are you sure?"

"Charge him double for the convenience fee," she said. And if it was who she thought it was, Shawn could afford the extra money.

"Great, thanks, Liss." Harriett left the kitchen, and Alissa got her industrial mixer going again. She'd barely filled her pitcher with warm water when the bakery manager returned.

"Uh...he wants you to deliver them. Says he wants to thank the chef personally."

"Who is it?" Alissa's heart started tapdancing in her chest. Would Shawn really come back and order so many doughnuts when she'd supposedly ignored him when he'd asked her to ride with him?

Didn't sound like Shawn. Of course, the man had matured a lot too. Had more muscles. Lines around his eyes.

"He wouldn't give his name. He paid in cash and left his address and phone number. I told him I'd text him if you could do that or not." Harriett looked worried. "He didn't look skeevy. Nice haircut. Blue board shorts."

"Gray T-shirt," they said together.

"I know who it is," Alissa said. "Can I have his number, please? I'll call him myself." And give Shawn a piece of her mind. *Fifteen dozen doughnuts.* She scoffed as Harriett wrote the number on a piece of paper and handed it to her.

After the manager had left, Alissa took the number and her phone outside. No need to make a scene where one of her sisters would overhear. But *fifteen dozen* doughnuts? Why couldn't the man just order what was in the case? Did he know how much work his insane order made for her?

"Shawn Newman," he said in an overly chipper voice when he answered her call.

"Fifteen dozen doughnuts?" she asked by way of a greeting. "Are you kidding me?"

"Bo's having a party at his place."

"Go to a different bakery."

"I want you to come to the party."

Alissa opened her mouth to say something, but nothing came to mind.

"I realize maybe I…I don't know. Moved too fast, asking you to ride in the parade with me. But you can't say no to a party at my brother's place."

Oh, she could.

She just didn't want to. A sigh filled her whole body, and she let part of it come out of her mouth. "Shawn, I don't know."

"What don't you know?"

"You live in Miami. Probably have a ritzy apartment. A private beach."

"Nope," he said. "Neither of those, actually."

"No girlfriend?"

The way he hesitated spoke volumes, and Alissa shook her head. "I can't believe I almost said yes."

"Lauren and I aren't defined," he said.

"I'm going to need more than that," she retorted.

"Okay," he said. "I'll make sure she knows we're nothing before the party tonight."

Once again, Alissa found herself without words. Well, she had one. "Why?"

Shawn took a few long seconds to answer. "Maybe I won't go back to Miami."

"Why?" she asked again. Surely he didn't have any lingering feelings for her. He'd *dumped* her for another girl.

"I don't know, Alissa." He sighed. "I just know I like being here. I liked seeing you yesterday. I want to see you again. Get to know you again, when I'm not full of idiocy and teenage hormones."

The parking lot on this side of the kitchen really smelled bad, and Alissa turned to go back inside. "Is that an apology?"

"Sure," he said. "I'm sorry for running off with Marcy in high school."

"So you do remember."

"Of course I do." His voice softened. "And I feel like an idiot about it. So come to the party. We can talk about the motorcycle ride another time."

Alissa couldn't believe what she was going to say. But no one needed to know. Olympia would flip out if she found out Alissa was hanging out with Shawn. Because she knew that thirty-five-year-old women didn't "hang out."

They dated.

"Fine," she said. "But do you really need fifteen dozen doughnuts?"

"Party's at six," he said. "And no, how about just two dozen?"

She wanted to throttle him at the same time she wanted to kiss him. The warring emotions inside her made her feel lightheaded. But at least she didn't need to stay and make doughnuts anymore.

"Bo's house?" she asked.

"Do you know where he lives?"

"Yes." She couldn't believe she did, but she did. Bo had never left the island, and he owned and operated a company that provided unique ways of transportation around the island. In the summer, they had a limit on the number of cars that could be on Carter's Cove, and most of those were taxis.

Bo rented scooters, bicycles, horse-drawn carriages, and golf carts out to travelers. He chauffeured them around if they wanted. It was a genius idea, and it wasn't uncommon to find his bright blue scooters outside of The Heartwood Inn on a daily basis.

"Six," Shawn said, a smile in his voice.

Alissa leaned against the metal door, a smile on her face as she said, "Six." Her very next thought was *What in the world are you doing?*

And honestly, she had no idea.

4

Shawn's nerves fired through him with the force of gravity. Lissa would probably take one look at him and the non-party at Bo's house and stalk away. He could just see her doing it, too. And dang, if that image didn't excite and terrify him at the same time.

When he'd first arrived in Carter's Cove, his goal was singular. Get Olympia Heartwood to sell. Why he'd thought he could actually do that, he wasn't sure. He hadn't known her well, as she was five years older than he and Lissa, well out of the house before Shawn even started high school.

She hadn't even remembered who he was until he mentioned his mother's name. Olympia knew Julie Newman, as his mother made all the floral centerpieces for big events at the inn. Still. She had for years, and The

Heartwood Inn had been her biggest client when Shawn was growing up.

He'd been such a fool, coming here with that proposal. His phone rang, and Jason's name struck fear behind his already clamoring heartbeat. He couldn't ignore his boss's call for a third time that day, though he wanted to.

He hadn't called Lauren yet either. Shawn wasn't sure what they were, but he thought they were past a break-up over the phone.

"Shawn Newman," he chirped into the phone, hating the sound of his own voice in that moment.

"Shawn." Jason's deeper voice carried all the fear it usually did, whether in person or not. "How are things going on the island?"

Shawn hesitated, though he knew his boss hated it. "Not well, sir," he said. "Olympia Heartwood refused to even discuss the acquisition of their inn and land."

"We need that land," Jason said. "Or our sprawling island getaway won't be so sprawling."

"I understand, sir," he said. "I don't think it's going to happen. The family has deep roots here."

"I don't understand," Jason said, and Shawn could just picture him standing at the wall of windows in his office, the ocean spread before him, the bodies on the beach mere dots below him. "You said money has a way of uprooting the deepest of feelings."

"I was wrong," Shawn said. Jason appreciated it when

someone admitted he was wrong. It was a tactic that had worked well for Shawn in the past.

Jason sighed, the sound meant to convey his displeasure, frustration, and impatience for Shawn. Nerves skipped through him, but he didn't know what to do about the situation. "I'm seeing a younger sister," he said, unsure of where the words had come from. "But I don't think it'll go well."

Especially because Lissa had already said they'd never sell. He didn't have plans to ask her again that evening during the non-party, but he couldn't very well tell Jason what his plans were.

He squirmed inside his own skin, wondering how he'd gotten himself into this situation. *Arrogance*, his mind whispered, and Shawn knew it was right. He'd been too sure of himself in the board room in Miami. But he didn't want Hunter to come up here and try to bully the Heartwood family into selling.

He'd volunteered, and he knew now that he'd known he'd fail the moment he opened his mouth in the meeting a month ago.

He sank onto the couch as Jason started talking. He said, "Yes, sir," and "Mm hmm," in all the right places, but he wasn't really listening.

"Yes, I'll let you know. She'll be here soon." Shawn got off the phone, because he hadn't lied. Lissa would be there soon, with twenty-four doughnuts they could never finish.

Shawn did love a good doughnut, and he'd shared many of them with Lissa while they were in high school.

She wasn't the same girl now that she'd been then. For one, she'd filled out in all the best ways possible. And number two, she didn't look at him with stars in her eyes. He wanted her to, but he liked that he had to work for it too.

Sighing, he picked up his phone again and dialed Lauren, hoping to smash the device into the wall afterward.

"Hello, darling," she said, and Shawn wanted to stab out his own eyeballs. She was probably on the beach or beside the huge pool in her daddy's mansion. He thought of Alissa, and wondered how in the world he'd ever been attracted to Lauren.

"Hey," he said brightly. "Listen, I hate to do this over the phone, but I just wanted to make sure we're...cool."

"Cool?" Lauren asked.

"You know, just friends."

A lengthy silence followed. When she finally said, "Of course. I'm going to dinner and the theatre with Seth tonight. So we're cool," he couldn't tell if she was angry or not.

Shawn blinked. "Seth Rotherberg?"

"That's right."

"You said you were just friends."

"Well, now I'm saying *we're* just friends." Lauren didn't

sound apologetic. Or upset. "Have fun in Carter's Cove, Shawn."

The line went dead, and Shawn stared at the device as the call faded from the screen. "Seth Rotherberg." The man worked for the Tremmel Group, of course. Most of Lauren's boyfriends did. Shawn knew that; had seen her date a few men before locking onto him.

Foolishness ran through him again, and he hung his head. "You're so stupid," he whispered to himself. What Lauren had thought he could do for her, he wasn't sure. But it had to be something, just like Seth could get her into all the sports functions around the city, because his brother was the quarterback for the Florida Falcons.

She'd already moved on. For all Shawn knew, she'd been snuggling up to Seth one night and going out with him the next.

He couldn't help feeling...something. Upset, maybe? Taken advantage of? Definitely foolish. Why he'd thought his relationship with Lauren was authentic when he'd been able to tell her others weren't, he wasn't sure.

Wishful thinking, he told himself as he silenced his phone. But now, he didn't have to feel guilty about his feelings for Lissa.

He couldn't even believe he *had* feelings for Lissa, but as soon as he'd seen her in that kitchen, dripping wet and red-faced, he'd started questioning a lot of his life choices.

A *lot* of them.

The doorbell rang, and Shawn jumped to his feet. How long had he been sitting there, thinking about Lissa Heartwood?

Too long, and he hurried to get the door. The star of his recent fantasies stood there, and wow, she was a vision straight from heaven. She wore a short little pair of white denim shorts with a navy blue top that hugged her upper arms and left her shoulders bare.

He could only stare, his mouth dry and his thoughts somewhere near the soles of his feet.

"Can I come in?" she asked, glancing over both of his shoulders. "Am I early?"

He stepped back quickly, coming to his senses. "Yeah, come in." The fruity scent of pineapple and mango came with her, and Shawn worked hard not to take in a deep breath of it as she passed.

"And funny thing," he said. "There's no party."

She turned back to him, her wedged sandals bringing her closer to his height. "There's not?"

"No," he said, deciding to get everything out in the open between them. "And I'm not seeing anyone in Miami, and I just wanted to...talk." Oh, he wanted to do so much more than that, but he could wait.

He'd have to wait, if the fear and surprise on Lissa's face was any indication. After taking the doughnuts from her and putting them on the kitchen counter, he faced her and gave a nervous chuckle. "So the party is just me and you."

"That's not a party," she said, folding her arms. "That's called a date."

"Okay," he said. "Whatever you want to call it is fine with me."

"I am not going out with you."

"We're not going out," he said quickly. "You brought the doughnuts with you."

Confusion puckered Lissa's eyebrows. "So that's it? We're eating two dozen doughnuts?" She took a step toward him, and it felt dangerous. He actually braced himself for the confrontation, his pulse rioting through his veins.

"I didn't eat dinner, because there's usually food at a party," she said. "And we're not going to be a thing."

"No?" He watched her, enjoying the indecision this time. "Why not?"

"You have a girlfriend in Miami."

"False," he said. "We broke up about an hour ago. In fact, I'm not even sure we were dating. She's going out with Seth Rotherberg tonight. She's probably been seeing him a lot."

Compassion filled her lovely eyes, but Shawn didn't need that. He shrugged, hoping the twinge of hurt wouldn't show. Just because he hadn't liked Lauren all that much didn't mean her betrayal didn't hurt. At the same time, they'd have had to been dating for her to betray him at all.

"We're not—you live in Miami. You're only going to be

here for a few weeks." Lissa sighed and stepped over to the doughnuts. "You know what? I do need one of these." She plucked a glazed doughnut from the box and took a big bite.

Shawn's hormones went nuts, and he'd been hoping to keep them subdued tonight. But watching her lick the glaze from her full lips? He was practically drooling—and not for want of a doughnut.

"Maybe we can just have fun for the next few weeks," he said. "No strings attached."

"I don't sleep around," she said. "I don't do flings." She took another bite of the doughnut, but her eyes never left his.

"That's fine," he said. "Neither do I."

Lissa chewed and swallowed, using that tongue to lick her lips again. The temperature was nearing astronomical though the air conditioner was pumping away. "Great." She walked over to the couch and sat beside Gentleman. "Hey, doggo." She ran her hands behind his ears, and Gentleman closed his eyes in bliss.

"Okay." Shawn couldn't believe that had gone that well. Something told him Lissa had some feelings for him too, and he snagged his own doughnut and sat on the other side of his dog, plenty of space between him and Lissa. Too much space.

"Remember when we ate all the doughnuts during the kid's carnival?" he asked. "Mrs. Goldman was so mad."

Lissa smiled and shook her head. "She should've been mad. There were four rounds of kids who couldn't do the doughnut contest because of us."

Shawn chuckled. "I'll take her that second dozen and apologize." He took a bite of the doughnut, a moan starting way down deep in his gut. "Liss, this is *so good*."

She grinned at him, that spark in her eyes she'd had when they were younger. "I can't believe you were going to make me make five more dozen of them."

"Sorry," he said after swallowing. "I won't do that again." He polished off his treat and stood up. "And hey, I found a bike for the parade. Want to see it?" He extended his hand toward her, actually surprised when she put hers in it.

A thrill ran through him as he pulled her up.

"I just want to say I zoned out a little yesterday," she said. "I didn't actually hear you ask me to ride in the parade with you." She squeezed his hand. "You realize that was our first date, right?"

"I'm aware," he said, gazing down at her. Before he could think too hard, he leaned down and touched his mouth to hers. Sparks and shocks traveled through him— and then he found himself stumbling back

She'd pushed him away.

Actually *pushed* him.

"Don't," she said, her voice angry now. "I can't believe —you broke up with your girlfriend an hour ago." A growl started down in Lissa's throat, and Shawn needed to rectify his blunder quickly, before she stomped out of his life for the second time.

5

Tears pressed behind Alissa's eyes, but she would not show them to Shawn.

"I'm sorry," he said, his electric blue eyes open wide. He seemed sorry. "I just lost my head. You look so beautiful, and I was just...I wasn't thinking."

"This is not a date," she said. "You're not my boyfriend. You don't get to kiss me."

"Got it." He nodded. "Sorry, Liss."

She loved how he called her the old high school nickname. She'd liked the feel of his hand in hers. And fine, she'd thought about kissing him too. But she wasn't actually going to do it. He'd leaned down and done it.

The awkwardness between them settled, and she said, "You were going to show me a bike."

"Right." Shawn practically jumped toward a door. "You'll never guess what it is."

"I'm not even going to try." She wanted to hold his hand again, but how would that look? Shove him away one moment, pull him in the next? She felt bi-polar and all over the place.

He led her out the back door into the small backyard. It looked good right now, but as the summer wore on and the heat baked the island, it would likely brown up. In the back of the yard sat a shed, and Shawn headed toward it.

He opened both doors to reveal an assortment of lawn tools—and a motorcycle.

Alissa pulled in a breath. "Is it the same one we rode?"

"Yes," Shawn said triumphantly. "I left it for Bo when I went to college, and he still has it. He says it doesn't run, and I haven't tried it, but I thought we could look at it tonight."

"I wouldn't have worn white pants if I'd known we were going to be getting mechanical."

"Oh, honey, those aren't pants." Shawn let his gaze drip down her gorgeous legs before looking at her again, one eyebrow cocked. "I'm sure I could loan you some clothes."

Her blood felt like someone had magicked it into lava. Heat licked through her whole body with the way he looked at her. He could certainly convey his interest without a single word.

She ducked her head, that blonde hair falling between them until she tucked it behind her ear. Her face felt overheated when she faced him again. "I'll hand you what you need."

"Deal." Shawn got to work extracting the bike from the shed and watching him use those muscles was almost as exciting as holding his hand. Her fingertips touched her lips, the ghost of his kiss there.

It hadn't even been a whole kiss. Just a touch. A press, before she'd come to her senses and pushed him back. Maybe she'd pushed a little too hard. She honestly wasn't sure what she was doing. Dressing up all cute, putting on lots of makeup and jewelry, and driving out into the suburbs of the island for a party that was really a date.

Then she hadn't left. She'd held his hand. No wonder he'd thought he could kiss her.

He swung his leg over the seat and just him sitting on that bike was the sexiest thing she'd seen in a long time. She could barely get her lungs to expand as he tried to start the bike. After several failed attempts, he said, "Yeah, this isn't going to start. Let's take a look."

He grinned at her, and she couldn't help smiling back. "Tell me what you do in Miami," she said as he pulled a toolbox out of the shed too.

"Okay, wow," he said, exhaling. "I'm a real estate investor by title."

"What does that mean?"

"It means I find undeveloped land in highly profitable places, buy it for the Tremmel Group, and they develop it. Make money on it."

"You had to know we wouldn't sell."

"I didn't suggest Carter's Cove," he said, arching one eyebrow at her before ducking his head to study the tools in the box. "When my associate brought it up, I volunteered to come. My boss let me, because I'm from here and he thought I could sway you."

"You knew you couldn't."

Shawn straightened, that smile so sexy on his mouth. "I knew I couldn't."

Lissa nodded, her emotions swelling and dipping all over the place. "Let's check the gas tank," she said. "Maybe it's just empty."

"DOUGHNUTS," SHE ANNOUNCED AS SHE ENTERED HER parents' house the next afternoon. Her dad's fishing boat was gone, which meant he wouldn't be there, but her mom and her grandmother both sat in the kitchen, a stack of cards between them.

"Alissa, dear," her mother said while Alissa held the door for her two dogs to enter. "Will you grab that notebook on the side table before you come over?"

Alissa detoured toward it and took it to her mom. "These are from yesterday, by the way. But they're still pretty good." Her non-date fixing the motorcycle with Shawn had been pretty good too. She hadn't asked him anything else about his job, but he did tell her about

Miami. She'd told him about her time in pastry school, and they'd eaten too many doughnuts while they laughed about the stupid things they used to do in high school.

He hadn't tried to kiss her good-night, though he had walked her all the way out to her car and held the door open for her while she got in.

She'd had a terrible time trying to fall asleep, that moment of gentle pressure from his mouth against hers a constant torment. In the end, she'd caught a few hours of sleep before heading out on *Big Blue* for the morning catch. Shawn hadn't put in any crazy baking orders, and now she was here for her regular Wednesday afternoon chats with her mom and grandma.

"Rummy again?" she asked as she took a semi-stale doughnut out of the box.

"We're nothing if not routined," her mom said with a smile. "You look tired, dear."

"I am tired." Alissa sighed. "I should go home and take a nap." After all, she worked seven days a week without an end in sight. She had someone she could call if she was too sick to go out fishing, and they had back-up bakers at the restaurant that could fill the cases if necessary.

Alissa loved her job, though, and she'd have to be one breath away from dying to take a day off.

"There's a new fried chicken restaurant going in," Grandma said. "You want to take me when it opens?"

Alissa grinned at her grandmother. "Of course I do."

"You work too hard, dear," her mom said as if that conversation was still going.

"Is Dad fishing?" Alissa asked, though she knew he was.

"Yes, and he went on a trip," her mom said, laying down a seven of hearts. "He won't be home until Saturday."

"We should live it up," Alissa said, standing up. "Let's make caramel popcorn and watch all the romantic comedies we can."

Her mother laughed, but Alissa wasn't entirely joking. She needed something to get her mind off Shawn, and something to keep her from texting him to find out what he was doing that day. She'd told him last night that she worked until one o'clock, and she'd been half-expecting him to text or call about then and want to get together.

He hadn't, and she hated how her mind had automatically gone to something untrustworthy for him. He'd never given her a reason not to trust him, except maybe the sudden disappearance from her life eighteen years ago because another cute blonde had shown interest.

As far as she knew, he and Marcy hadn't even lasted until the end of senior year. But he hadn't come back to her, and Alissa had figured out how to stop thinking about him once. It sure seemed impossible now, though.

She filled a big bowl with water and set it on the floor for Dodger and Pirate, who'd taken up protective positions around Grandma. She loved dogs, and they loved her, and Alissa's heart warmed just from looking at the three of them.

"Do you have popcorn, Mom?"

"Are you serious?" her mom asked. "You brought a dozen doughnuts with you."

"What about dinner?" Alissa asked. "You want me to make you something?"

"There's already a casserole in the oven." Her mother played another card, and Alissa was grateful for the rummy game that kept her mom from focusing on anything but it.

"Okay," Alissa said, returning to the table. But she couldn't sit still. If Shawn was going to only be here for two weeks, she wanted to see him every day.

Her mind screamed the word *traitor!* at her, but the need to see him remained. She couldn't call him, though. Olympia would be livid, and Alissa reminded herself that Shawn was a visitor to Carter's Cove. He didn't have unlimited vacation days, and he'd go right on back to Miami.

And she'd stay here.

"Deal me in," she said to her grandmother as her mom squealed gleefully, all the cards coming together in suits from one to twelve.

"That's another one for me, mother," she said, marking it in the notebook.

"Who's ahead?" Alissa asked.

"I am," Grandma said.

"But I'm catching up to her one game at a time."

"Will I throw you off if I play?" Alissa asked. Because she could not sit here and watch the two them. Not today.

"Of course not, dear." Her mom smiled at her. "Now, what's got you so restless?"

"Nothing," Alissa said.

"Probably that man from Miami," Grandma said, and Alissa's gaze flew to her.

"How do you know about the man from Miami?" she asked.

"Olympia called the other day," her mother said as she shuffled the cards. She could do it without looking, which impressed Alissa. She dealt too, never taking her eyes from Alissa's. "I think it's definitely a man."

"No." Alissa shook her head. "No man. No boyfriend. Nobody. I'm just tired today. I don't want to just sit here and watch you two play."

"What happened with that guy?" her mom asked. "Olympia said she asked you to take care of him."

"I told him we weren't selling." Alissa shrugged. "He left the hotel, and now he's staying with his brother." She cursed herself and her loose tongue.

"Oh? He's still here?" Her mom didn't miss much. Even when Alissa thought she wasn't paying attention, she was.

"It's Shawn Newman," Alissa said. "Didn't Olympia tell you that?"

"No." Her mom paused in her play, her eyes zeroing in

on Alissa again. "The Shawn Newman you dated in high school?"

"Yes."

"The one who broke your heart?"

"He didn't break my heart, Mom." Alissa added an eyeroll to the statement, because her mom was closer than she knew.

"Alissa, please." Her mom shook her head. "You were distraught for months after he broke up with you."

"I was?"

"Don't you remember? Daddy and I told you if you didn't pull yourself together, we were going to have you go see someone. You graduated, and moved away to school, and you seemed so much better."

"I don't remember that." Alissa searched her memory for what that talk would've looked like, sounded like. It didn't exist in her mind, but of course, she couldn't remember a whole lot from those last few months of high school.

All at once, she knew why. She *had* been in a funk. She *had* been distraught over the break-up. She pushed the thoughts away and focused on the cards in front of her. She never seemed to get what she needed, and she didn't understand how her mother and grandmother played this game every day. Their boredom had to be higher than hers.

Thankfully, Grandma went out pretty quickly, and Alissa stood up. "Okay, I'm going to go catch a cat nap with the pups. Come on, guys." She leaned over and pressed a kiss to Grandma's forehead and hugged her mother.

Once free of the house where she'd grown up with four sisters and only one bathroom, Alissa sat behind the wheel, wondering where she could go that wasn't back to the cottage.

The ringing of a bell filled the air, and she knew she wasn't going anywhere. The roads would be jam packed with people, as that bell had just signaled the start of happy hour.

Carter's Cove had dozens of little festivals throughout the summer, and this afternoon, all the local restaurants and pubs were hosting a mini food and wine festival. The streets would be packed with people moving from one storefront to another—The Heartwood Inn included.

She sighed, tired of this internal war and it had only been raging for a couple of days—since Shawn had walked back into her life.

Without thinking, she picked up her phone and called him. It might have been a mistake, but if he'd been working on the bike today, maybe he could come pick her up and they could navigate the crowds on that motorcycle....

6

Shawn hadn't been this dirty in a long, long time. He actually liked it. Liked the way he felt like he'd accomplished something that day. Yes, he'd had to pull apart the motorcycle until dozens of parts were strewn over the dropcloth he'd laid on the ground.

But the bike started. It needed more than just a tune-up to be rideable in the motorcycle parade, as the locals who participated in that—and the hundreds who came to the island in the days leading up to the Fourth of July—had pristine bikes they spent a year getting ready.

Shawn had nine more days. Thankfully, his father had raised him with a Mr. Fix-It attitude, and Shawn knew he could get the bike looking amazing in time. He couldn't help thinking about the woman he wanted leaning into him as they cruised down the narrow streets of the island.

He wondered what Lissa was doing this afternoon.

He'd stopped by the bakery in the morning for his day's carbohydrates, but he hadn't seen her. He didn't need to see her to find her in the tasty treats in the bakery case in the lobby of The Heartwood Inn.

He could taste her in the black forest cupcakes. The woman loved cherries and chocolate together, and he smiled just thinking about the time she'd challenged him to eat a dark chocolate covered cherry. He'd never tasted anything as disgusting in his life, and she'd laughed and laughed.

Kissed him and kissed him.

He'd been so stupid, letting her go. Cutting her loose. Truth be told, both of those were nicer than what he'd done to Lissa. One rose and a couple lines from a blonde, and he'd abandoned their eight-month-old relationship.

Yes, they'd been kids. But he wasn't that guy. Well, he supposed he had been once, and he'd regretted it ever since.

His phone rang, and he reached for the blue mechanic rag he'd bought at the automotive store that morning—the second stop after the bakery. "Hey, Liss," he said. "I was just thinking of you."

"Yeah?"

"Yeah, I got the bike started. Wondered if you wanted to go for a ride."

"You don't know what today is, do you?"

"Uh, Wednesday?"

She giggled, and Shawn's mind blanked. "It's the food and wine tasting downtown."

He groaned. "So we can't get out of town. Wait. Where are you?"

"I'm at my mother's," she said. "I was thinking...you'd come get me on that bike and be able to zip us through the crowds and cars to dinner."

Surprise lit up his face, his brain now firing with ideas. Possibilities.

"We could walk the streets from your place," he said.

"Exactly," she said. "And later tonight, when the hype has died down, you can bring me back to get my car."

"Sure," he said, looking at his disgusting hand. It seemed ten times dirtier now that he was thinking about holding Lissa's hand with it. "I need a few minutes to clean up and find some helmets."

"I'll start walking down the street a little," she said.

"You don't need to do that. I'll come get you."

"I don't want my mom to know."

He almost asked *Know what?* but he caught himself in time. She didn't want her mother to know she was seeing him again.

The call ended, and Shawn went inside Bo's house to get cleaned up. Gentleman went out to sniff around, and Shawn watched him, wondering what it would be like to not have to worry about a relationship.

Were he and Lissa seeing each other? Maybe they were just hanging out, like last night when she'd come over. They'd talked about Miami and Carter's Cove, eaten doughnuts, and looked at an old motorcycle. Was that a date?

Was walking down a crowded street and sampling short ribs and street tacos? He wouldn't be kissing her, that much was obvious. Any contact between them would come from her, just like last night.

And she hadn't touched him.

They were definitely not dating. Not seeing each other. They were friends. Friends hanging out, enjoying the summer festivities on the island where they'd both grown up. There was nothing wrong with that.

With his hands as clean as they were going to get, he strapped a helmet to his head and started for her mom's house. Lissa was only about three blocks away from her mom's, walking slowly with her phone up in front of her face.

She lowered the device when she heard the motorcycle, and a grin split her face. For a moment, Shawn saw the girl he'd crushed on for six months before asking her to ride with him in the motorcycle parade.

"You got it started," she said, coming over to the curb. She had more curves now. Her hair only touched just below her shoulders. But her eyes were still the same. Still bright blue and able to see things he didn't want her to know.

"Yep," he said, swinging his leg off the bike and handing her a helmet. "You want to go get your dogs?"

"They'd love to get out," she said. "But that means we can't go inside any of the restaurants or pubs."

"That's okay with me," he said. "We can sample on the street and still get full."

She finished buckling the helmet on, and he climbed back on the bike. She swung her leg over the seat behind him, nearly knocking him off the bike.

"Sorry," she said, laughing a moment later. He joined in, because it was so easy to be with her. So carefree. She didn't get embarrassed if she couldn't do something, and he liked that she could laugh at herself.

"All right," he said. "Ready?" She wasn't touching him, but her body was so close to his every nerve stood at attention.

"Ready," she said, and he eased the motorcycle into motion. It didn't want to seem to go with their combined weight, and he opened the throttle a little more.

Suddenly, the bike shot forward. He yelped at the same time Lissa did, and in the next moment, her arms snaked around his torso. "You did that on purpose," she said, her voice loud and clear in his ear.

"I did not," he said. "She wouldn't go." But he wasn't complaining. The way Lissa pressed into him was a sensation he hadn't experienced in a long time, and he didn't want to arrive at her house anytime soon.

Unfortunately, the ride from her mom's to her house didn't take long, even though they had to go down the busiest street in town. He just went slow, and people got out of the way, until he could make the turn that would take them back to the beach where her cottage was.

"Are all your sisters still on the island?" he asked as they got off the bike and de-helmeted themselves.

"Yes," she said. "We all have an active part in running Heartwood."

"Let me see if I can guess."

She grinned at him and gestured for him to go right ahead. He followed her into the house, where her dogs barked and wagged their welcome to her. She got out leashes as he said, "So Gwen's the youngest...my best guess is she runs the spa in the hotel."

"Nope," Lissa said, obviously enjoying the fact that he was wrong.

"So Olympia runs the whole empire," he said. "You run the boat and the bakery."

"How did you know about the boat?" she asked.

"Please," he said. "You've always loved that boat more than life itself. Your parents are retired, so there's no way your dad's getting up at three o'clock in the morning to go fishing."

She gave him a curious look he couldn't quite decipher before turning back to her dogs. She clipped their leashes to their collars, and faced him. "You'll want Dodger. He's much more obedient."

He took the leash she gave him, and sure enough, Dodger sat right down at his feet. The dog looked up at him, his eyes wide and puppied, as if to say, *Aren't I great? Do you have a treat?*

Shawn chuckled at him and scrubbed behind his ears. "This one needs a treat."

"Right there." Lissa pointed to the counter behind him, and he grabbed a handful of the beef and salmon bites. He fed one to Dodger and put the rest in his pocket for later.

"You haven't guessed anyone else," she said.

"I don't know," he said. "You were my friend in high school."

Her eyebrows arched, and an electric rush moved through Shawn. Surely she felt that too. Or maybe she was the one doling it out. "I mean, we were more than friends, obviously."

She simply looked at him, and he knew a man could get lost in the depths of Lissa's eyes. He cleared his throat and looked away. "You tell me what they do."

"Gwen runs the restaurant." She sounded a bit breathless too. "Celeste does all the marketing and events. All the weddings, anniversaries, stuff like that. And Sheryl does all the grounds. All the interior design. Anything that requires maintenance, she's your girl."

"Do you like it?"

"I love my role," she said, heading for the front door again. "Should we go?"

He followed her out, the afternoon sun hot as they walked back the way they'd come on the motorcycle. The cottage was only a couple of blocks from the downtown area, but it sure was quiet out on the beach.

"Play City is here," she said, pointing to a bright yellow food truck at the end of the street. "I definitely want to stop there."

"I'm not familiar with Play City," he said, peering down the street.

"Yes, you are," she said, bumping him with her hip. "They do the crazy doughnuts. You got the candied pig once."

How she remembered that, Shawn had no idea. He honestly didn't. But he said, "Okay, if you say so," and veered toward a woman handing out something that smelled like smoked meat.

They talked and sampled. She laughed at him when he spit out the jalepeno poppers, and he shook his head when she refused to try the catfish jelly.

About halfway down the block, Lissa got bumped too close to him, and he grabbed onto her arm to steady her.

"Sorry," he said quickly, removing his hand from her skin. Their eyes met, and so many things were said between them.

"It's okay," she said, inching away again. "A mistake."

Shawn pressed his lips together and took a deep breath, wishing he could turn his brain off. But it was now screaming at him that maybe he could be her boyfriend by mistake. Just for a little while.

They could hold hands by mistake.

Watch the clouds make patterns in the sky by mistake. Kiss by mistake.

Wait. He'd already done that, and a slow smile curved his lips. Lissa wasn't looking at him and didn't see, but she did turn to him and say, "Shawn, you've got to try these prawns. They're *fantastic*."

And he went right over to her, because she was gorgeous and full of life, and everything he'd been missing in his life.

7

Alissa enjoyed her time on *Big Blue* the following morning. She loved the way the water talked to the boat and the big catch she was able to bring in. Gwen grinned at her in the restaurant, and she didn't even mind the morning meeting they had to remind everyone about the picnic that afternoon.

Another of Carter's Cove's traditions, Picnic Day actually took place on the beach—which happened to be right out the back doors of The Heartwood Inn. They'd have all their sea kayaks, surfboards, and wakeboards out for rent, along with beach umbrellas and chairs.

The beach would be filled with people from noon on, and Alissa wanted to get in the bakery and get her treats made so she could text Shawn and arrange to meet him. The very fact that he was there, inside her mind, ready to be seen again, frustrated and excited her at the same time.

"We sponsor this event," Gwen said, as if the restaurant staff didn't know. "So we'll have our potato skins on special all afternoon. Five dollars, and I need four extra people on apps this afternoon." She called names while Alissa flipped her phone over and over, trying to decide how she felt about Shawn.

He'd backed way off about buying Heartwood, but she wondered if that would last. He still had his real estate development job, and he wouldn't just give it up. Not only that, but he'd spoken true. It wasn't his firm out of Miami, which meant he had a boss to report to. Would that boss really just take no for an answer? Who would he send next?

"Liss, can we also offer something from the bakery?" Gwen asked.

"I don't see why not," she said, tuning in quickly. "Why don't we do a special? Get people into the bakery. Cupcakes at buy one, get one half off?" She could make a lot of cupcakes. "Reduce our inventory of other items and focus on those. Cupcakes are very picnic and beach friendly."

"I like it," Gwen said, and Alissa nodded, her workload shifting away from kneading and rising to baking and frosting.

The meeting broke up, and Gwen grabbed her arm. "Who was that guy you went to the food festival with yesterday?"

"The one Olympia wants me to keep occupied until he

leaves town," she said. That much was true. No one had to know how much she was enjoying herself by keeping Shawn occupied.

"He looked familiar."

"He's a Newman," Alissa said, wondering if Gwen would remember that Alissa had actually dated Shawn. She was five years younger than Alissa, and twelve-year-olds didn't really care who their older sister went out with. Gwen had just wanted Alissa to get out of the bathroom faster and stay out of her bedroom.

"Oh, right," Gwen said, but Alissa could tell the name didn't mean much to her.

"Darryl's your age," Alissa said.

"Oh, duh. Darryl Newman." Her face lit up with recognition. Someone called her name in the next moment, and Alissa felt like she'd dodged a bullet.

She tied her apron around her waist and got mixing up cake batter in droves. With the huge trays and industrial ovens, she'd made a thousand cupcakes by lunchtime, as well as a few other things to stock the bakery cases for the day.

When she finally pushed out of the kitchen and into the sunlight, her fingers felt like she'd been squeezing a stress ball for hours. She flexed them as her eyes adjusted to the brighter light out here.

"Hey," a man said, and she jumped away from the voice, her fight reflexes kicking into gear.

"Whoa, it's me," he said, and the voice finally registered in her head.

"Shawn?" She lifted her hand to shield her eyes from the sun. It was Shawn, and he wore the same pair of blue board shorts, this time with a yellow T-shirt. "What are you doing back here?"

"Got lost," he said, though she didn't really believe him. "It was a mistake." He brushed her hand with his as he passed her. "Oops. That was too." He grinned at her and kept moving through the small parking lot here, stepping onto the sand a moment later.

Alissa watched him, sure she was about to make the biggest mistake of her life by following him. But riding that motorcycle with him had been the most amazing thrill of her year, and that was simply pathetic.

"Are you going to Picnic Day today?" she asked.

"Yes," he said over his shoulder. "Are you?"

"I was thinking about it."

"Maybe we'll bump into one another on accident," he said, and she decided to let him go. Everything he'd said had been cryptic, but loud and clear at the same time.

She'd bumped into him yesterday and called it a mistake. He'd just waited outside the kitchen entrance for who knows how long. That wasn't a mistake. Neither was his hand touching hers. And them running into each other later would definitely not be a mistake.

In fact, Alissa was going to make sure she "ran into him" on the beach. She smiled as she started toward home, ready for a shower and to get something to eat that wasn't composed of mostly sugar.

By the time she left the house again, she wore a bright blue bikini beneath a white coverup, a pair of flip flops that weren't functional but were definitely flirty, and a big, beach hat that the wind tried to steal right off her head.

She'd left Dodger and Pirate in the house, but she carried an oversized beach bag on her shoulder. Towels, check. Sunscreen, check. Snacks, check.

Now all she needed to do was find Shawn. He hadn't texted or called, and she hadn't ever spent this particular day with him. They'd started dating at the motorcycle parade, and that was still eight days away.

Bodies and brightly colored umbrellas already filled the beach in front of her, and for a moment, she considered just doing straight down to the shore she owned. No one would pass the orange cones, as that marked the Heartwood private property, and while tourists could sometimes be rude, they respected the boundaries ninety-nine percent of the time.

She paused on her front porch, the scene before her overwhelming. If she wanted to find Shawn, she could be an adult about it and text him. No games.

"Be honest with him," she muttered to herself. Playing games had gotten her in trouble in the past, and she really didn't need drama this summer. No, she just wanted someone to spend her lazy afternoons and evenings with, and Shawn was the perfect body for that.

She didn't need serious, and that made him all the better of a candidate, because he didn't live here. He'd leave, and she could go back to her real life, her family, and her job.

But while he was here...she didn't see why they couldn't hang out.

Thirty-five-year-olds don't hang out.

She knew she was right, but her fingers still moved over the screen on her phone. *Hey, where might I bump into you?*

As soon as that text went through, she typed out another one. I'm thinking we can hang out and have fun while you're here. Nothing serious. No strings, like you said.

She stared at the words as the circle spun, and then they were delivered. She couldn't get them back even if she wanted to. And she didn't want to.

I'm coming to get you, he texted back, and Alissa looked up from her phone, her heart suddenly tap dancing in her chest. She went down the steps and into the sand, thinking she could at least meet him out in the public area.

She'd no sooner crossed the line onto the public beach when he emerged from behind a rainbow-colored umbrella several feet away. A smile touched his mouth, and he lifted his hand as if she couldn't see him.

Alissa felt like she'd only had eyes for him for eighteen years. She pushed the thought away and waved back.

He stepped right into her and hugged her with a, "Hey.

I was wondering how long it would take for you to come out."

"Where are you?"

"Down here a bit." He stepped away and started back the way he'd come. "I just ordered pizza, and it should be here soon."

"You ordered pizza on Picnic Day? Don't you know you're supposed to *pack* a lunch?"

"Is that what you have in your bag?"

"I mean, I have snacks."

"What kind of snacks?"

"Nothing you like." She smiled up at him, glad her sunglasses allowed her to look up into his face. "What kind of pizza?"

"Meat lovers with green peppers."

Alissa nodded like that was a normal order, but she knew it wasn't. "Just like when we were kids," she said.

"It's been my favorite since you introduced me to it," he said.

She stopped just before entering the mass of bodies. "Shawn, I just have to know. This is just...casual, right? We can be friends while you're here."

She couldn't see his eyes behind those shades, but she saw the sly smile as it formed on his mouth. She couldn't look away from that mouth, even as the body it was attached to crept into her personal space.

"Sure, Lissa," he said, his lips right at her ear as he slid one arm around her waist. His yellow T-shirt smelled like coconut oil and sunshine and sand, and she wanted to breathe in that manly scent for the rest of the day. "We can be friends while I'm here." He touched his lips to her skin right below her ear and backed up. "Sorry. That was another mistake."

He ducked around the umbrella, leaving Alissa stunned and frozen in place. Heat filled her again, and then again, and after several seconds, she let the thrill of his lips touching her skin flow through her too.

"Not a mistake," she said to herself as she rounded the umbrella too, finding Shawn several yards down the beach but waiting for her. "And he wants to be more than friends."

Problem was, so did Alissa. As she flipped and flopped her way through the sand, she couldn't decide why they couldn't be.

He doesn't live here, her brain reminded her.

And he dumped you for Marcy without a second thought, her heart said.

He apologized for that, her mind countered. And back and forth her thoughts and her pulse went, so that by the time they arrived at the spot of beach he'd claimed, Alissa felt utterly spent.

She'd set down her bag and pulled out a towel when another man approached with the pizza.

"Ah, yeah," Shawn said, taking the food from him and handing him a twenty-dollar bill. "Thanks, man."

He turned toward Alissa, a gleeful smile on his face. "Let's eat."

She wanted to do that. She wanted to soak up the hot rays of the sun. She wanted to relax. And maybe, just maybe, she wanted to hold Shawn's hand.

8

———

Shawn sat down on the blanket he'd found in Bo's closet and then spread over the sand. He'd rented an umbrella from Celeste, who hadn't seemed to recognize him, which was honestly fine. She wasn't the Heartwood sister Shawn was interested in.

And he'd been sitting on the beach for an hour by himself, wondering how he could get Lissa go come join him. In the end, she'd texted him, and he couldn't help feeling like she didn't really want to be "just friends" while he was here.

"Pizza," he said, handing a slice to her after she spread out her towel and sat down.

"Thanks." She flashed him a smile, and added, "We should go get some cupcakes later. They're on sale today."

"I saw the sign," he said. "How many did you make?"

"A thousand," she said like it was no big deal. Like

normal people whipped out that make cupcakes on the daily.

"Wow," he said. "And you want to eat one?"

"They're good," she said, and he watched her take a bite of her pizza. The movement made something in him fire that hadn't in a while, even with Lauren, and Shawn couldn't believe he'd been living his life in black and white in the most vibrant city in the world.

He took a bite of his pizza too, simply so he'd have something besides Lissa to focus on. "Who's the band tonight?" he asked after he'd swallowed the cheesy goodness.

"This local group called Lowcountry," she said.

"Fitting."

She watched the waves as she ate, and Shawn wondered if she'd allow them to have a relationship. He'd been pretty forthright in what he wanted without coming out and saying it. So maybe he should do that.

"I'm thinking about staying in Carter's Cove," he said, deciding the back of the guy's head in front of them was the safest spot to look.

"What?" Lissa practically screeched the word, and Shawn had to look at her.

Words started building beneath his tongue, but by the look on her face, his statement was not welcome news. "My job is boring," he said. "My life there is dull. I don't know." And he didn't know what he'd do.

Jason hadn't called again, which had honestly

surprised Shawn. Jason would give Shawn a few days, and then he'd want to know how his "meeting" with the younger sister had gone. He wasn't the type of man who knew how to take no for an answer, but Shawn knew he would not be working on trying to get Alissa to sell.

The Heartwood Inn was so much more than land. It was their family's legacy, and he'd been so far removed from that type of situation in Miami, he hadn't even known it. If he had, he'd have talked Jason and Hunter out of this particular piece of property from the beginning.

"I'm just not sure I want to go back," he said.

"You have a job there," she said.

"So I'll get a job here."

"There's no real estate to develop here, Shawn. The whole island is...." She waved her hand in a swirling pattern. "Developed."

"I have other skills," he said coolly. "Why does this upset you?"

"Because." She sighed and looked away. She gazed down at the pizza box, where she snatched another slice.

"Maybe you do have flings," he said. "Or maybe you're worried we won't just be a fling."

"I *don't* do flings," she said, cutting him a glare without truly turning to look at him. "And we're not anything, nor are we going to be."

"Why not?" he said.

"I don't make the same mistake twice."

"Maybe it's not a mistake."

Lissa didn't answer, and Shawn decided to really drive his point home. "Liss, even if it is a mistake, I kinda want to make it."

She shook her head, her mouth set in an angry line. He reached over and touched her knee, then her arm. She just looked at the spots where his fingers had landed, her eyes finally moving to his. Though they both wore sunglasses, he felt like she had to be able to see his sincerity.

"Plus, I don't think it's a mistake, us meeting again like this."

"You came to steal my family's inn."

"No, I came to *buy* it, which by the way, you should be grateful you got me and not Hunter Reynard." He sighed, not wanting to fight with her. Fighting *for* her was just as hard though.

"That sounds like a threat."

"I'm not trying to argue with you," he said. "Look, why did you text me today?"

She took a bite of pizza, her jaw moving angrily as she chewed. Shawn gave her the time she obviously wanted, though it drove him crazy.

"My sister asked me to keep you busy," she finally said.

Shawn blinked as the sharp edge of her words dove into his heart. "Okay, wow." He stood up, not sure how he'd read all the signals wrong. He also didn't know how to get his blanket out from under her, as she'd placed her towel partially over it. The umbrella had to be back by ten p.m., but she could take it.

"Shawn," she said, but he couldn't stay for another second.

"I'll be back," he said, but he didn't know if that was true or not. He headed down toward the water's edge, his eyes trained on the line of couples waiting for their turn on the water trikes. He needed a second person to actually maneuver around the course, but he wasn't going to go back and beg Lissa to be that woman.

He'd begged enough, that was for sure. The woman had an iron fist of denial around her heart, he'd give her that. And fine, he was only in town for eleven more days anyway. It wasn't like they were going to fall in love by July sixth.

Can't you? The voice pinged around in his head, but it only fueled his anger, propelling him past the line and down the beach.

"Shawn," Lissa called again, and he slowed down. She caught up to him a few seconds later, her breathed ragged.

"I just got hot," he said, making himself as bad of a liar as she was.

Lissa darted in front of him and held up one hand. A little boy ran behind her, shouting something as his sister chased him. Shawn didn't want to have this conversation here, but Lissa wore a look of determination in the line of her lips.

"I don't—I'm sorry," she said, deflating slightly and lowering her hand. "I didn't mean what I said back there."

"Which part?" he challenged.

"The part where I said Olympia asked me to keep you busy."

Some of the fury dissipated, but he still felt steamed. His thirst drew him toward a teenager pulling a red wagon full of ice and bottles of water. He pulled a five out of his pocket and handed it to the kid, taking two bottles from the wagon with a "Thanks."

He handed one to Lissa, who just watched him. "So why did you text me today? And call me yesterday. If you weren't keeping me busy, what were you doing?"

She ducked her head, and if Shawn could see her eyes, he'd have his answer. As it was, he still felt like he was guessing when he said, "I think you like me, and you want to spend time with me, but you're scared."

"I am not," she said, that familiar fire coming back into her voice.

Shawn chuckled, though he didn't feel entirely happy. "So what is it then?"

"You're really pushy, you know that?"

"Well, you're just as stubborn as you've always been."

She rolled her whole head, and he laughed, because he knew it would irritate her.

"I just got out of a pretty serious relationship," she said. "And I don't—I just want fun this summer."

"Sounds dangerously like a...." He leaned closer,

feeling the sparks flying from her body and kissing his. "A fling."

"It wouldn't be a fling," she said quietly, their faces almost nose-to-nose.

"Then what would it be?"

"If you go back to Miami, it'll just be fun."

"The kissing kind of fun?"

"Maybe," she said, and Shawn's heart stopped beating. He blinked, blinked, and then his pulse raced forward again.

"And if I stay on the island?"

"Then it gets complicated," she said. "And I don't want complicated."

"Fine," he said, straightening, and taking a breath that wasn't full of Lissa's sugary sweet scent. "Then I'm going back to Miami on July sixth. You get your eleven days of fun."

She started back toward the umbrella where their pizza waited, and Shawn could only hope and pray that he'd get his version of fun in the next eleven days too.

"THEY WERE REALLY GOOD," HE SAID LATER THAT NIGHT, the darkness on the beach absolute once they'd left behind the bright spotlights that had been pointed at the stage.

"Yeah, not bad," Lissa said, walking through the sand

better than Shawn did. Admittedly, he normally wore polished shoes and worked in an office, while she lived on the beach. He'd noticed that she'd ditched the flip flops and tucked them in her bag after about five steps, though.

The rest of the afternoon had gone well. They didn't talk about his job, or hers, or anything about their relationship. They finished the pizza, and ate cupcakes, and talked about everyone they'd known in high school, all the happenings around the island for the next eleven days, and then they'd listened to Lowcountry, the fun, hipster band that had combined bluegrass with rock.

And now he was walking her home. Shawn knew better than to expect a kiss. Number one, she hadn't even held his hand that day. Number two, he'd tried kissing her once already and gotten shoved. He wasn't going to do it again, especially since Lissa had six steps leading to her front door.

"Thanks for walking me home," she said. "It gets dark out here."

"Yeah," he said, noting the flimsy excuse. After all, she got up and went fishing alone at three o'clock in the morning. He supposed she did have her dogs with her, but it still felt like a weak reason to keep him with her for just a little longer.

Maybe Shawn was delusional. He didn't know. What he did know was that he liked spending time with Lissa when they weren't arguing. When they were navigating through the buoys, trying to keep their trike upright and on track. When they could eat chocolate and laugh about the past.

But it wasn't the past on Shawn's mind as he stood on the porch with her. It was the future, and if she could be in his.

Eleven days, he told himself. And then he'd go back to Miami, as promised. If he didn't do that, he couldn't even have Lissa for eleven days.

"Thanks for a great day," she said with a smile. "I'm going to seriously regret it tomorrow." She reached for the doorknob but paused.

He didn't even have time to inhale before she wrapped her arms around him and hugged him tight. "Maybe tomorrow we can just go watch the dog show in the evening?"

Shawn slowly put his arms around her too, trying to memorize the feel of her there. She fit—she always had. "Sure," he said. "What time does that start?"

"The agility course is my favorite," she said, stepping back. "It starts at six. Then I can take a nap after work."

"Six," he repeated, his mind feeling sluggish from her touch. "I'll come get you on the bike about five-thirty then."

"Five," she said with a smile. "I want time to get one of those garlic and cheese sausage rolls. They *only* have them at the dog show."

Shawn grinned, a laugh not far behind. "I've forgotten about those."

"They're still amazing," she said, shifting her feet as she set her bag on the porch. "Anyway, see you tomorrow." She tipped up on her toes and swept her lips along his cheek, bending to get her bag and opening the door in the next second.

Shawn watched her enter the cottage and close the door behind her, and still he couldn't move.

This woman was going to be the death of him, and he realized he might not survive the next eleven days if she was going to hug him and then tease him with a kiss as chaste as that.

He turned and went down the steps, picking up the blanket he'd brought from Bo's. His brother had texted no less than six times, but Shawn had ignored him. Just like he'd ignored the call from Jason when it came in about eight p.m.

His boss would still be up, and Shawn dialed him as he headed for the sidewalk that would take him back to the parking lot and the motorcycle he'd been driving around the island.

"Shawn," Jason said, his voice perfectly pleasant, without a trace of exhaustion in it.

"You called?" he asked.

"Just seeing how things are going with the Heartwood project."

"They're not," he said. "Look, Jason, I told you this in Miami—we'll be lucky to get this land."

"I don't remember you saying that."

He stepped from Heartwood property to city land, and he paused. "They're not going to sell. I can feel it down in my gut."

"Do I need to send Hunter?"

"If you want," Shawn said as he turned around. Down the lane sat another house, and Lissa had said Celeste and Gwen lived in that one. "But the project is going to have to be altered. We're not getting this land."

Jason sighed, the sound displeased. "I'll start looking at other areas. You should do the same. I want a new plan and proposal on my desk before you go on vacation tomorrow night."

"Yes, sir," Shawn said, a twinge of guilt pulling through him. He was supposed to be working this week—and he had been. On a motorcycle. On his tan. On getting Lissa to break down her walls.

He reasoned that he had all day tomorrow to find Jason another patch of Earth to purchase, and if there was anyone who could do that, it was Shawn.

"I also heard you and Lauren aren't seeing each other anymore," Jason said, and Shawn's heart stopped for the second time that day. This time, it actually hurt, and he searched for something to say.

"No, sir," he said, hoping he'd made his voice an appropriate level of sad. "She wasn't that interested in me." He swallowed, his tongue suddenly thick. "And she had a thing going on with Seth Rotherberg."

"Yes," Jason said, his disapproving father voice making

an appearance. "She has been pictured with him recently. Well." He exhaled, and his voice was bright when he said, "I'm sorry it didn't work out."

"Me too," Shawn said, because on some level, he was.

"Email or fax," Jason said. "New plan and proposal by five tomorrow."

"You'll get it," Shawn said. After all, he had a date with Lissa at five tomorrow, and he couldn't blow her off for work.

9

Alissa made it through her work day without nodding off, but if she had a desk job, she'd have been asleep by noon.

She managed to make it home and back into bed before falling asleep, a dog on both sides of her. She'd set her alarm for four so she'd have time to shower and get ready before Shawn arrived at five.

Instead of waking to a peaceful chirping noise on her phone, she bolted straight up in bed when Dodger and Pirate started barking. They jumped from the bed and streaked out of her bedroom, leaving her alone with her rippling heartbeat.

"Hey, guys," Shawn said, and true panic gripped Alissa's lungs. "Liss?" he called, and Dodger came running back into the bedroom.

"No," Alissa said. "Get out of here, Dodger."

But he simply jumped up on the bed and faced the door, panting with that smile on his face. Pirate barked, and Shawn said, "All right, all right." His tall frame filled the doorway, where he stalled.

"Hey," he said.

"Hey." She had no choice but to respond, but she couldn't get out of bed. She only had a T-shirt and underwear on, and while that might be more than the bikini she'd worn yesterday, this felt completely different.

"My alarm obviously didn't go off," she said, reaching for the phone on her nightstand. "What time is it?"

"Five," he said.

Her heart swooped down to her stomach, and when she blinked, her vision went completely black.

"I'll wait out here," he said, despite Pirate's body right behind him. He backed up and then stepped forward to grab the doorknob so he could pull it closed, giving her some privacy.

"What the heck?" she muttered to her screen. The alarm was set, but she hadn't clicked *Save*, which meant it wasn't actually on.

She set the phone down, took a big breath, and pushed her hands through her hair. No time to shower. That was fine. She threw the covers off and stood up. Ten minutes later, she had her hair in a ponytail and her favorite lip gloss on her lips.

Out in the living room, Shawn sat with Pirate in his

lap, holding his phone above the dog's head. "Pirate," she said. "Down."

The dog obeyed instantly, and she added, "You don't have to let him invade your space."

"I liked it." He got up and scanned her, licking his lips as his eyes met hers. "You look great. I was going to say we don't have to go tonight if you're tired."

"I've been asleep for three hours," she said, smiling, glad her cutoffs had done the job she wanted them to. The purple tank top she'd chosen usually did too, and it was nice to know Shawn wasn't immune to her.

Problem was, she wasn't immune to him either. As she'd told herself last night and again all morning as she'd fished and baked—it wasn't a problem. *She* was the one making her attraction to him an issue.

She just needed to let go, get out of her own way. Enjoy the time with him. Ten days now.

"And I'm starving," she said, putting one hand against his chest. "You aren't getting out of buying me dinner, Mister."

"Wouldn't dream of it," he said, capturing her hand in his and holding on. Alissa pulled in a breath but she didn't pull away. "But we are going to be a little late."

"We should be okay," she said. "Sorry about over-sleeping."

"I don't mind," he said. "I don't care what we do at all." He sounded like he was telling the truth, and Alissa grinned at him.

This time, when she got on the bike behind him, she didn't hesitate to wrap her arms around his midsection and lean into his back. He took off, maneuvering them up into the neighborhoods instead of going through town to get to the park.

He pulled up to the valet, though surely they wouldn't allow a motorcycle to take the space of a car. "Hey, Bo," he said, and as Alissa took his hand to let him help her off the bike, she realized he was talking to his brother.

"Shawn," he said, nodding to a guy behind him. "And you must be the woman who's kept him busy for me."

She stilled, sure Bo was digging at her. Shawn looked horrified, and he made a swiping motion with his hand as if to say, *I swear I didn't tell him anything.*

Alissa forced a laugh out of her throat as she removed her helmet and shook out her hair. "I suppose I am," she said. "Good to see you, Bo."

"Alissa?" He looked back and forth between Shawn and Alissa. "Oh, this is going to be a great story." He didn't seem to notice the car that had pulled up behind them, nor the golf cart.

"Are you still dating Anna?" she asked, though she knew he was. Just because there were thousands of tourists here didn't mean the locals couldn't keep up with gossip.

"Yes, he is," Shawn said, handing the keys to another valet. "Thanks Gene. See you later, Bo." He grabbed Alissa's hand and practically pulled her away from his brother. He didn't keep hold of her hand, and Alissa couldn't help laughing.

"He looked like you'd grown an extra head." She giggled again though he was headed straight for the garlic and cheese sausages.

"Yes, well, I'm sleeping on his couch, if you'll remember. He thinks he gets to know where I am all day and what I'm doing."

"He doesn't?"

Shawn reached the line and slowed to a stop. As soon as she stepped beside him, he took her hand and lifted it to his lips. "No," he said. "No one gets to know."

"Not even me?"

"You're with me," he said.

"Not all day," she said. "What did you do today?"

"Nothing," he said, looking away, the sure sign of a lie.

She scoffed and pulled her hand away. "No hand-holding if you're going to lie."

"Fine," he said, reaching for her again. "I went to the bakery, hoping to see you when you brought out another tray of brownies or something, but you stayed stubbornly in the kitchen. Then I went to breakfast by myself, did some work for my firm, and then I sat outside your place until the clock ticked to five."

He sighed in such a way that told her how insufferable he found her. "Happy now?"

"Yes, actually." She squeezed his hand. "I'll bring out the trays of brownies tomorrow."

"I would appreciate that."

"How long did you sit outside my house?"

"I'm not answering that," he said. "I need to keep some of my pride." He inched forward when the line moved.

Alissa couldn't help laughing, cuddling into Shawn's chest as she did. He received her willingly, keeping their fingers intertwined and putting his other arm around her waist. "And you know, that rule goes both ways."

"What rule?"

He stepped back, disentangling all of his limbs from her, and she instantly mourned the loss of his touch. "Telling the truth or there's no love."

She folded her arms and cocked her hip, but Shawn only chuckled. "What have I lied about?"

"Fine, maybe you didn't lie," he said. "But, Liss, I don't want to spend the next several days talking about who we were. I want to get to know who you are now."

"Fine," she said.

He moved forward again, and she came with him. "You start," she said. "Favorite food now that you're thirty-six-years-old."

"Hey, you'll be thirty-six in two months."

"I'm aware," she said coolly.

"Six weeks, actually," he said.

"Favorite food," she said again, but now all she could think about was having him on the island with her to celebrate her birthday.

"Tacos," he said. "Favorite fish."

"Halibut." She stepped forward and ordered for both of them. "Favorite drink," she said, turning back to him, enjoying this game a little too much. But he knew not to ask the typical favorites, the way she was. He knew she adored fish, and she wondered what he'd ask next.

"Ginger ale." Shawn took her hand in his, pulling her away from the ordering window so they could wait for their sausages. "How many times a week do you nap?"

"Several," she said. "How many hours a week do you work?"

"Sixty or seventy," he said, flinching slightly as the words as they came out of his mouth. She wondered why, but he asked, "What are we going to tell your sister?" and all her thoughts jumbled.

"What?"

He nodded over her shoulder, and Alissa spun around to find a very angry-looking version of Olympia walking toward them.

"Let me go talk to her," she hissed at the same time the guy in the sausage truck called her name.

"I'll get them," Shawn said. "That looks like a hurricane, Liss." He moved away from her, and Alissa faced her sister. She wanted to ask Shawn why he always used her nickname when no one else did. Ask him if he was really thinking of staying here in Carter's Cove. Ask him if he'd stay if she asked him to.

But right now, she had to deal with Olympia, who marched forward and grabbed Alissa's arm as if she wasn't already going to go with her. "Hey," she said, wrenching her arm away. "What is your problem?"

"You're dating him?"

"No," Alissa said quickly. "You told me to keep him away from Heartwood, and that's what I'm doing."

"I saw you holding his hand. Snuggling into him."

"So what?" Alissa challenged. She wasn't a teenager, and Olympia wasn't her mother. "He's not going to buy Heartwood, and that's what's important."

"No, what's important is that you don't let him soften you up."

"You're being ridiculous."

"Am I?"

"Yes," Alissa said. "I'm not having this conversation here."

"Look—"

"No, Olympia, you look." Alissa usually got along with all of her sisters, but she felt so hot for some reason. "Just because your last boyfriend was married and lying to you doesn't mean every man is like that."

Olympia sucked in a breath, her eyes going wide. Alissa's anger faded, and she fell back a step. "I'm sorry," she said quietly. "I didn't mean that. It's just...Shawn's only here for a few more days, and...."

"And you like him," her sister said.

Alissa didn't want to admit it out loud, especially to Olympia. "Can I come see you tomorrow after work?"

Olympia looked away, her anger now raging into indecision.

"O, I'm not an employee," she said. "You don't have to play the tough guy with me." Alissa put her hand on her sister's arm, and when she didn't jerk away, Alissa drew her into a hug. "I'm sorry I said that about Hunter." But that guy was a real jerk. He had been technically married when he started dating Olympia, and then once his wife had figured things out and left for Hawaii, he'd married a different girlfriend.

Olympia had really been through the presses in the past few years, and Alissa usually made life as easy as possible for her sister. She did have a loud bark, but that had gotten worse after Hunter, and as her responsibilities at The Heartwood Inn increased.

Olympia sniffed and stepped back. "Sorry to interrupt."

"It's fine," she said. "We're just hanging out. It's nothing serious." Maybe she'd been thinking of kissing him tonight. But she couldn't now, not when she'd just said they weren't serious.

10

Shawn watched Lissa hug her sister, and the older woman in the professional pantsuit walked away, straightening her hair and looking around. Liss stood still for a few moments, and then she turned, already searching for him.

He lifted one of the sausages he'd collected from the pick-up window, and she started toward him, those tan legs making his blood run hotter with every step. "Sorry about that," she said, accepting the cardboard tray with her sausage in it.

"It's fine," he said. "Everything okay?"

"Yes."

"What was she upset about?"

Lissa looked over her shoulder in the direction Olympia had gone. "She's had a rough time of things lately," she said, facing him again. "And she thought you were playing me." She lifted her sausage to her lips, taking a great big bite of it. A few onions and peppers fell back into the tray as she tried to smile and chew at the same time.

"I'm not playing you," he said.

She finished and swallowed. "I know that." She nodded toward the entrance to the park. "Let's go."

Shawn gestured for her to go on ahead, and she did. He fell into step beside her, his curiosity nearly choking him. But he wasn't going to ask again. He and Lissa were getting along for once, and he wasn't going to rock the boat.

"Favorite ice cream flavor?" he asked her, hoping they could pick up their game where it left off.

"Oh, come on," she said, nudging him with her elbow. "You know that one."

"Hey, it could have changed."

"It hasn't."

"Cookies and cream is so *boring*, though," he teased.

"Well, we can't all like spumoni or pistachio," she said, her tone dry.

He laughed, pulled out a couple of bills to pay for their entrance to the dog show, and they started toward the arena where the agility course had been set up. A cheer went up from the crowd, and Lissa hurried forward, turning backward as she danced on her toes.

"Come on, we're going to miss it."

Shawn chuckled as she reached for his hand and they jogged the last few steps to enter the stands. She led them to some seats near the end of the course, and she handed the cardboard tray to Shawn when she finished, as if he was the designated holder of trash.

He honestly didn't care. Watching the dogs complete the tasks was exciting, and sitting beside Lissa was enough to keep his blood pressure near the top of the charts.

"I hope Rafael wins," she said, her eyes on the chart on the other end of the field.

"There are still a few dogs left," he said, wishing he'd gotten a drink with his sausage. Because all this yelling for canines had really made him parched.

The next pup came out, and it moved fast. "Uh oh," Shawn said. "I'm rooting for this one."

"Oh, come on," Lissa said, bumping him with her shoulder. "You can't be a fair-weather fan. I'm rooting for the underdog."

"Well, Magic is going to cream him." He stood and started clapping, cheering for Magic as he raced up the ramp and hit the mark exactly right. "He's amazing," he said.

"Sit down." Lissa pulled on his shirt. But Shawn went on cheering, and Magic crossed the finish line ahead of Rafael's time.

Shawn whooped, and when he sat down next to Lissa she gave him a sour look. "Don't be a sore loser," he said, threading his fingers through hers. She laughed and leaned her head against his shoulder.

In the break between dog runs, she said, "Okay, big dream you haven't done yet."

"Run a marathon."

She accepted his answer and looked at him for his question. "Same question," he said. "Big dream."

"To own my own fish shop."

He turned fully toward her, the moment between them very real and very vulnerable. "Really? I would've chosen the bakery for you."

"Nah," she said. "I love the boat. I love fishing. If I could, I'd buy that little storefront next to the flower shop. You know the one right on the corner as you come into town? And I'd sell my catch there every day."

"Then what would your family do for fish?"

"They can buy it from me." She laughed, and Shawn smiled at her. She may have tried to play things off lightly, but he knew she really would fish every morning and stand behind that counter with the iced catch in front of her, ready to sell to whoever came through the door.

"My turn," she said. "Favorite song."

"Finding Roots," he said.

"Country? Really?"

"Hey." He shrugged. "It's better than that classical stuff you listen to."

"It is not. And that *classical stuff* is very peaceful when I'm out on the boat in the morning."

Shawn snorted, and then he squeezed her hand.

"What are the chances I can join you on the boat one morning?"

She sobered, and Shawn liked the fun, playful version of Lissa, and this more serious one as well. "You want to come out on the boat at three in the morning?"

"Sure, sounds fun."

"You never thought it sounded fun before."

"Yeah, well, I was seventeen before," he said, a touch more bitterness in his voice than he intended.

The next dog came out of the gate, and he was a streak as he ran down the field. "Oh, Magic is going to lose," Lissa said.

Shawn thought she was probably right, as this dog hit every turn exactly right—until the cones. He zigged and zagged—and missed a flag.

A collective "ohhh," went up from the crowd, and the dog corrected itself and continued on. Shawn couldn't help cheering along with everyone else as he finished the course, and he still barely came in after Magic.

"Phew," Shawn said as if he really cared which dog won this contest. "That was close."

"I get up at three," Lissa said out of nowhere. "Leave at three-fifteen. If you're late, you get left behind."

Shawn smiled to himself. "What does one wear when shrimping at three-fifteen in the morning?"

"Whatever one wears to bed," she said with a smile.

"Oh, come on," he said. "I'm pretty sure you don't wear pants to sleep, so that can't be true."

She gasped, and Shawn laughed, and she hit his bicep. "I wear pants to sleep."

"Uh, is that why you wouldn't get out of bed this afternoon when I showed up?"

"That was a nap," she said. "And you're scandalous."

He shook his head, chuckling. Shawn couldn't help his fantasies, but he didn't speak them out loud. "I'll put pants on when I wake up," he said.

She scoffed, and the last dog shot out of the gate. Shawn watched, cheering despite himself, and Trixie won the whole thing with a perfect performance.

Lissa was still talking about the dogs as Shawn walked her up the sidewalk to her cottage. She opened the front door and Dodger and Pirate came sprinting out, both barking as they did. They ran off into the darkness, and only the weak porch light illuminated him and Lissa.

"Thanks for a great night," she said, finally facing him. She kept her hands tucked in her back pockets as she smiled coyly at him.

He didn't move a muscle. "What are the chances of us having some of the fun I want to have tonight?"

"Oh, you want a kiss, is that it?"

"A man can dream." He ducked his head, as all of his dreams lately had featured Lissa.

One hand landed on his chest, and that was a very good start to this new fantasy. But then Lissa ran her fingers along the side of his face, and back into his hair, and he realized this was no fantasy.

She came halfway, and Shawn put his arms around her and closed the distance between them, this kiss far superior to any of the others they'd shared. She matched his movement, seemingly just as excited to kiss him as he was her, and because of that, he pulled away long before he wanted to.

"Was that a mistake?" she whispered, both of her hands behind his neck as she practically hung on him.

"Not even close," he said, dipping his head to kiss her again.

WHEN SHAWN WOKE, HE COULD BARELY PRY HIS EYES OPEN. He couldn't believe Lissa did this every day, seven days a week, all year long. He knew she didn't take days off. Such a thing would mean higher costs as the restaurant bought their fish from a commercial establishment for the day. And if there was anything the local island restaurants prided themselves on, it was fresh fish caught daily.

He realized that his alarm was not going off. But something had woken him. Something like a chime or a ring.

His phone flashed with a blue light, and he reached for it at the same time it rang. That was the sound he'd heard, and he saw Jason's name on the screen, along with the numbers 2:11.

"Two o'clock in the morning," he grumbled as he unplugged the device and swiped on the call.

"Yeah?" he asked.

"Good, I woke you," Jason said.

Shawn didn't see how that was good, but he didn't argue. "What's going on?"

"There's been some vandalism over at the build site. I need you to go check it out."

"Okay." Shawn got out of bed and looked down at the gym shorts he wore. Did he really need to put on a suit to go out in the middle of the night? Deciding against it, he simply pulled on his shoes, grabbed the keys to the motorcycle, and headed out.

The engine made such a roar in the quiet night, and Shawn felt bad as he navigated the sleepy streets to the high-rise hotel the Tremmel Group had been building for four months. It was only about three stories high right now, but it was supposed to be fifteen. No one on the island had liked it, so the vandal really could be anyone.

A police officer met him and asked, "Are you Shawn Newman?"

"Yes, sir." He pulled out his wallet and showed his ID. "My boss said there was some vandalism? He wanted me to find out everything I could."

"Back here." The cop led him into the structure, where there were plenty of unfinished walls, plastic hanging over things, and the scent of dust and metal hanging in the air.

The hair on Shawn's arms stood up as he navigated through the dark maze, his creep-o-meter pinging off the charts.

"There," the cop said, pointing to where another officer stood with the construction team lead. Shawn had met with Ron the first day he'd come to town. The two men shook hands, and Shawn looked at the words spray painted in red on the cement.

Stop building.

You're ruining our beach.

"What area of the hotel are we in?" he asked.

"This is going to be the kitchen," Ron said. "The ovens will go here. You can see the drains for the dishwasher and sinks and things." He aimed his flashlight on the ground, though it wasn't so dark that Shawn couldn't see them.

"Do we have cameras or anything on the build site?"

"No, sir."

"Any leads?" he asked the cops.

"The only other thing we found was this." The first cop led him over to the outside door. "This door was locked, but it's clearly where they entered from." He indicated the metallic marks that looked like someone had clawed back the door with something strong.

The police officer went outside, and there, on the other side of the door, sat a single red heart, neatly painted around the door handle.

Shawn pulled in a breath, but he told himself that anyone could've done this. Just because there was a heart here didn't mean one of the Heartwood family had done this. Besides, the only options in that family were women, or a seventy-year-old man who liked to fish.

He gave himself a mental shake. None of Lissa's family had done this. They couldn't have.

At the same time, he knew he wasn't going to be making a three-fifteen launch time on her fishing boat, and he quickly pulled out his phone to text her that he couldn't make it that morning.

Exhaling, he turned around in a circle. "Did you search out here?"

"What do you think we'd find?" the cop asked.

"I don't know." Shawn took a few steps away from the door. "The item they used to get it. A spray paint can. Something." There only seemed to be upturned buckets and a lot of construction supplies. A pallet of rebar and bags of cement.

He turned back to the building, realizing how far he'd gone. The cop stood there, a dubious look on his face. "They're not going to leave such obvious things behind," he said. "But I can have a couple of guys search around back here if you want."

"Thank you," Shawn said. "And in every room in the building. We want to make sure there aren't any other instances of vandalism." He'd been on other builds that were controversial. This wasn't the first time he'd witnessed vandalism. He just hadn't realized such a nasty thing would occur on Carter's Cove.

Everything about the island spoke of home to him,

and while he'd promised Lissa he'd return to Miami, he'd been planning to go for a day or two and then come back. Just long enough to pack all the essentials in his apartment and put it up for sale.

He sighed as he lifted his phone to his ear, Jason's number all queued up.

"There's more up here," an officer called, and Shawn lowered his phone without dialing. This was going to be a very long night, and he was supposed to have the rest of his time in Carter's Cove as vacation.

He didn't think that was going to happen now, and he wished Lissa was awake so he could talk to her about it.

11

Disappointment cut through Alissa when she woke and saw Shawn's text that he wasn't going to make it. He hadn't said what had come up, only that something had. It could literally be anything, from his alarm going off and him chickening out, to him meeting another blonde and going home with her.

"He didn't do that," she told herself as she switched out her pajama pants for a pair of jeans. Shawn had grown and matured a lot in the past couple of decades, and she had to let go of Marcy at some point.

She filled a bottle with water and headed out onto the porch. She couldn't help looking down the sidewalk as if she'd see Shawn's motorcycle there though he'd said he wouldn't be able to make it.

The sidewalk remained empty, just like it had been forever at this time of day. He had texted only a half an hour ago, and she thought about calling him as she walked down to *Big Blue.*

In the end, she didn't. He'd texted. She didn't need to be clingy or jealous or whatever she'd be if she called him. Desperate. Yeah, she didn't want to come across as desperate.

"Board up," she said to the dogs, and they jumped onto the vessel. The engine groaned as she always did before turning over, and Alissa set out into the cove.

Her mind never moved far from Shawn, and she was surprised at how quickly he'd become part of her normal thought patterns. Of course, that bone-melting kiss last night had certainly helped to establish that.

She pulled in a good catch that morning, and she got started on the day's baked goods as normal. Every time a tray needed to be taken out to the storefront, Alissa did it, always searching the patrons for Shawn's sandy blond hair and wide shoulders.

Finally, about mid-morning, as she pushed through the swinging door with a tray of carrot cake, she met his eye. A flush filled her face, and she almost dropped the cakes. Harriett helped her steady them and she took the tray to slide it into the refrigeration unit.

Alissa wiped her hands down her apron, though it was dirtier than her skin. She moved quickly around the bakery case to the table where Shawn sat. "Hey," she said, sliding into the chair opposite him. He wore a suit on a

Saturday, and if that wasn't odd enough, he hadn't smiled once at her.

"What's going on?"

"I have to go back to Miami early," he said, delivering the words with careful precision.

The air left Alissa's lungs. Something stung behind her heart, but she didn't know why. *She* was the one who'd just wanted to "hang out" and "have fun." She didn't want serious. Hadn't they said no strings?

"Oh," she said, hoping to give herself a few more seconds to find composure. "For how long?"

He flipped over his phone as it made a noise and checked the screen. He picked it up and tucked it in his inside jacket pocket, so much like the real estate investor he was. "I'm not sure." He met her eyes again, finally softening into the man she'd been spending time with this week.

"I also wanted to apologize in advance."

"For what?"

"There was some vandalism at the hotel my firm is building." His eyes were so serious they barely looked like they belonged to him. "I had to give the police everyone I thought would have a grudge against us, or the building."

His words plowed into her with the weight and speed of a runaway train. She fell back against the chair rungs. "You think I vandalized your building?"

"Not you, specifically, no," he said.

"You think one of my sisters did that?"

His eyes said no. He even shook his head. But his mouth said, "I don't know, Lissa."

Alissa was not good at hiding her emotions, so she was fairly certain the anger and annoyance mingling inside her showed on her face. "So you turned us in."

"I gave the cops your name," he said. "I expect someone will contact you or Olympia."

"My name specifically?"

"The Heartwood Inn," he said.

She leaned forward, pressing her palms against the cool table when she felt so hot. So hot. "Newsflash, you arrogant fool. We don't care about your high-rise hotel. People come to The Heartwood Inn for a family atmosphere with resort luxury."

He reached across the table, his touch hesitant. "I know that, Lissa. I just...I had to give the police any and all information."

She pulled her hand away, though her nerves zinged at his touch. "You need to stop calling me Lissa. My name is Alissa."

"Liss—" He cut himself off, pure resignation on his face. "Can I call you when I get to Miami and know more?" He stood up and picked up his coffee. "I really don't think you did it. I don't want this to come between us."

She stood up too. She wasn't even sure there was an "us," but she knew she'd wanted there to be. She hadn't wanted to admit it, but the truth had a way of burning through her whether she acknowledged it or not.

"Sure, call me," she said, because she didn't want to lose him. And she did need to know how the investigation went as the police searched for who'd vandalized the high rise. "I'd love to stay up-to-date on the investigation."

"Lissa." He shook his head. "Sorry, I just can't do it. I can't call you Alissa. That's not who you are to me." He took a step toward her, crowding into her personal space. A smile finally touched that mouth, and he leaned down and pressed a chaste kiss to her lips. Nothing like what they'd done the night before.

Mere hours ago, actually.

"I'll call you," he said. "My flight leaves in a couple of hours, and it's murder getting off this island."

She couldn't help smiling at the joke, though it was an old one and she'd normally roll her eyes. After stepping back, she let Shawn move past her. Watching him walk to the exit was an exquisite form of torture, and just when he was about to leave, she called, "Shawn?"

He turned back, his eyebrows up.

"Where are the keys to the motorcycle?" she asked, striding forward. "I'll work on it while you're gone."

Hope brightened his eyes, and he said, "I left them at Bo's. He doesn't lock his doors." He kissed her again, lingering a little longer this time, and then he left.

Alissa stepped out onto the sidewalk and watched the

morning crowd swallow him, hoping he really would come back for the motorcycle parade in just one week. And boy, she had a lot to do before then if they were going to ride that bike together and be able to hold their heads high afterward.

A FEW HOURS LATER, WITH THE BAKERY CASES FULL AND Shawn surely off the island, Alissa walked through the expansive lobby and down the hall toward her sister's office. Olympia lived on the top floor of the inn, only renting out the other suite up there to extreme high rollers for an exorbitant amount of money.

She stepped into the administrative offices, but Olympia's usual secretary wasn't there. Only the Heartwood sisters worked seven days a week, so Alissa stepped past the usual gatekeeper and knocked on her sister's door.

"It's Lissa," she said, startling at her own use of the nickname she hadn't called herself in so long.

"Come in," Olympia called from within the depths of the office. Alissa pushed into the space, and Olympia looked up from something on her desk. "Morning, Alissa." She seemed perfectly pleasant this morning, and Alissa wondered what had truly set her off yesterday. It couldn't have been Alissa holding hands with Shawn.

"Hey." She sank into one of the plush chairs in front of the desk.

Olympia closed the folder and set it aside. She wore jeans today, with a cute red peasant shirt. That was about as casual as she got, and Alissa nodded to the shirt. "I like your shirt."

"Thanks." Her sister sat behind the desk. "Are you dating Shawn Newman again?"

"Sort of," Alissa said.

Olympia smiled and scoffed at the same time. "Come on, sis."

"I guess I would say we're dating," she said. "It just sort of happened by mistake."

Olympia's eyebrows vented down and then lifted. "So he's your boyfriend by mistake."

"Right," Alissa said. "Has anyone from the police come to talk to you?"

"The police?" Alarm entered her face. "Why would the police come talk to me?"

Alissa told her about the vandalism at the high rise, and everything else Shawn had told her. She ended with, "So he went back to Miami to see what his firm is going to do. He said he'd call me when he had more information."

Olympia remained thoughtful for a few moments. "The only one I can see who might even do this is Gwen."

"O," Alissa said. "No way. Gwen acts tough, because she's got all those meathead chefs trying to railroad her." She shook her head, shocked her sister would think Gwen could break into private property and deface it. "She didn't do this."

"We wouldn't sell to them."

"And Gwen didn't even know the offer was on the table. Only we did." She pointed between herself and Olympia. "*I* didn't do it. Did you?"

"Of course not."

"And I'm pretty sure Granny wasn't out in the middle of the night with a can of spray paint."

Their eyes met, and Olympia chuckled. Alissa did too, and soon enough they were both laughing hard.

Olympia finally took a big breath and wiped her eyes. She was always put together so perfectly, but Alissa knew she carried a heavy load for their family. "Okay," she said. "So I'll have to deal with the police. Did Shawn tell you what the vandalism was?"

"He didn't say anything about it," she said. "It wouldn't look good for us if we knew, right?"

"Yeah." Olympia looked at her phone as it flashed. "I can't believe you're dating him again."

"I can't either," Alissa said honestly. "It's kind of surreal. I liked him so much in high school, and I was devastated when he dumped me for Marcy Myers."

"I know you were, sis." Olympia smiled at her. "Mom and Dad were planning an intervention."

Alissa wanted to roll her eyes. Instead, she felt the love of her family stemming back decades. It filled her, and she stood up so she could escape in case the tears made an appearance. "All right," she practically sighed. "All this evening activity has exhausted me. I'm going to go let the dogs out and take a nap."

"Lucky," Olympia said. "Keep your phone on. If the police call me, I want you here for the interview."

"Okay." Alissa opened the door and left, glad she'd finally admitted to one person that Shawn was her boyfriend—even if it had happened by mistake.

Outside, the sun baked the island, which was fine with Alissa when she wore a bikini and had something cold to sip. But walking home along the beach in the summer heat wasn't her idea of a good time.

Once in the coolness of her house, she texted Shawn. *Hope you arrived safely. Call me when you can.* She put a heart emoji on, and then took it off.

She wasn't in love with him.

"I hope he comes back," she said to Dodger, and she wondered if she could add that to the text before she sent it. Trying to avoid appearing desperate, she sent the text as-is and climbed into bed.

No alarm needed today, as she was once again back to her quiet, boring afternoons and evenings with only herself for company.

Yes, Shawn had definitely made Alissa's life more interesting, and she put up one more plea that he would come back to Carter's Cove. Why she was so worried about it, she didn't know.

"Please," she whispered. "Let him come back to the island...to stay for good."

12

Shawn waited until everyone else had deplaned before he stood up and collected his carryon luggage. He didn't want to be here in Miami, and he prolonged the moment as long as possible.

But he couldn't stay on the plane, so he got off, nodding to the flight attendants as he did. He'd almost forgotten where he parked or what his car looked like. He'd almost forgotten the way from the airport to his apartment, and he almost forgot which floor he lived on.

He found his way home, though, and he stood just inside the closed door, a sigh leaking from his lips.

Jason would expect him within an hour, but Shawn didn't want to wear his rumpled suit he'd found wadded up in the corner of his suitcase and tried to steam all the wrinkles out of with an appliance that barely worked.

He hadn't showered this morning, as Bo had been in

when Shawn needed to leave. He hadn't been back to sleep since the phone call at two a.m. and exhaustion rolled through his shoulders.

A hot shower would perk him up, and Shawn left his suitcase by the door as he headed for the bathroom.

Half an hour later, he knotted a fresh tie around his throat, grabbed his wallet from the kitchen counter, and headed out again.

Jason's secretary stood when Shawn got off the elevator, and he was surprised to see the woman in the office on a weekend. "He's waiting for you."

"Thanks, Helen." Shawn gave her a smile, though dread filled his stomach. He opened the door and entered the office. "Jason." He strode forward and shook Jason's hand, nervous now that he was face-to-face with his boss.

"Any updates?"

Shawn wasn't sure how he was supposed to get updates while he was twenty thousand feet in the air. "Nope," he said. "You know everything I know."

"I know a bit more," Jason said, his tone bordering on arrogance. "Hunter was on the island with you."

Shawn didn't know what to say. He managed to stumble over to one of the plush chairs in front of Jason's desk and sit down. "You sent Hunter after me?"

"Of course not," Jason said, his features hardening. "You're my best guy, Shawn, you know that. Yesterday afternoon, when we got your report, he suggested he go to the island to talk to Barbara and Rich Saddler, because you said they had land we might be able to get." He rounded the desk and sat in the chair beside Shawn.

"It was a good alternative, and you were starting your vacation." Jason shrugged. "The Saddlers said no too." He threw up both hands as if to say, *So that's that.*

"Do we think it was the Saddlers who did the vandalism?" Shawn asked, thinking of the spray painted heart on the exterior door.

"I don't know," he said. "Hunter's on his way back here too, and we're going to let the local police handle it."

Shawn wanted to text Lissa right now and let her know, but by some strange will, he didn't reach for his phone. "And the project?"

Jason sighed. "I honestly don't know about that either. There's no way it can be what we storyboarded, and I've got a call out to the Hilde Group. They might not even be interested if all they have is a hotel crammed on an island with dozens of other hotels."

Carter's Cove was so much more than that, but Shawn didn't say anything.

"So." Jason groaned as he got up. "I've got two more properties for you to look at now that you're back." He collected a couple of folders from the corner of the desk and extended them to Shawn.

Dumbfounded and unsure of what to do, he took them. He didn't flip through them like he normally would have, because he didn't care about the properties inside. He didn't want to go back to business as usual, because after only five days, he didn't care about this business anymore.

He wanted to return to the island, the woman, and the easiness of the beach. Of course, he'd need a job there, but jobs weren't in short supply on Carter's Cove. Every business needed more help, especially during tourist season, and Shawn had plenty of money saved from his years in the suits, the corner office, the real estate developing.

Back in his own office, he sat at his desk, a place he used to be so comfortable. Now, it just felt like the wrong place to be. He was wearing the wrong clothes, and he lived in the wrong city.

He pulled out his phone and called Lissa, but the line just rang and rang. Frustrated, he didn't leave a message when her recorded voice came on the line.

Sighing, he stood up and moved over to the window. He used to love this view, but now it was of the wrong beach. Determined to go back to Carter's Cove and be with Lissa, he turned, almost tripping over his own feet at the sight of Hunter in the doorway.

"Back already?" Shawn asked. He had no problem with Hunter, other than the man acted like the smartest in the room no matter what was being discussed. Sometimes arrogance like that could take a person far, but Shawn thought Hunter could dial it down a notch or two.

"Yeah." Hunter closed the door behind him and moved toward the chairs in front of Shawn's desk.

"I was just leaving," he said, not wanting to entertain his co-worker right now.

"Where are you going?" He tapped the folders Shawn had thrown on his desk.

"It's Saturday," Shawn said, dodging the question. "And I was supposed to have the next two weeks off."

"Hm." Hunter sat down, obviously not going anywhere. "Shame what happened to that hotel on Carter's Cove." But he didn't sound like he felt bad about it.

Shawn sat down, narrowing his eyes at Hunter. "What did the Saddlers say?"

"About what I expect the Heartwoods did." Hunter gave him a cold smile. "But they'll be battling each other now."

Shawn cocked his head, trying to hear more than what Hunter had said. "The families on that island are very loyal. They have deep roots. I told you that."

"You said money would uproot anything."

"I said *almost* anything," Shawn shot back. Embarrassment filled him that he'd once thought that. There were so many more important things than money. How had he allowed himself to forget that?

"Well, we'll see what happens next."

"What do you mean?" Shawn stood up as Hunter did.

"I mean, the Heartwoods are suing the Saddlers for vandalism."

"What? It wasn't even their hotel that was hit." If

anyone had a legal complaint, it was the Tremmel Group, and Jason wouldn't do that. Not for a few scrawled letters in red paint. He'd clean it up and move forward. Hire a guard to watch the building.

"The heart on the back door...I guess Olympia Heartwood took offense to that. Said the Saddlers were trying to frame them. It's gotten ugly there. Glad I got out when I did."

Shawn had only left that morning. Could things have really gone downhill so fast? He clenched his teeth, because he didn't want to say anything else in front of Hunter.

"I need to go," he said, his voice tight.

"Yeah, go." Hunter walked toward the door. "And if you talk to your girlfriend, tell her I said hi." He flashed a monster smile and walked out, leaving Shawn frozen behind his desk.

If he talked to Lissa?

And how did Hunter know he was dating her? If he'd only been on the island since last night, he wouldn't have had any way of knowing. And why would Hunter be talking to her at all?

"Come on," he said as he pulled out his phone and jabbed at Lissa's name on the screen. "Answer the phone, Liss."

But she didn't, and Shawn barked a message onto her voicemail. "Can you please call me back as soon as possible?"

He wasn't sure what was going on, but he knew he didn't have to work today. He fled the building in favor of his apartment several streets over, and still Lissa didn't call him back. She could be as stubborn as the day was long, and Shawn remembered the way she'd let him kiss her for half a heartbeat before shoving him away.

That was all her stubbornness right there, and he hoped just like in that instance, she just needed some time to come around. Then she'd call, and he'd find out what was going on and how he could help.

Let me know what I can do, he texted as he rode the elevator up to his place. He'd stepped inside, a sigh falling from his lips, when a woman said, "There you are. My father said you'd be back today."

"Lauren." Shawn froze with the door open still. "What are you doing here?"

"Well, Seth's busy this weekend." She smiled flirtatiously as she prowled toward him. "I thought maybe we could talk. Get coffee."

Shawn didn't want to talk or get coffee. "I'm seeing someone else," he said.

"That's okay," Lauren purred. "So am I."

He shook his head. "No, Lauren. This is serious." As soon as he said it, he realized how serious about Lissa he was.

"Please, that blonde from the beach? You've known her what? Five days?"

"We—how did you know she was blonde?"

"Oh, Hunter sent me a picture." She waved her hand as if that was a stupid question. "You know she's a shrimp boat captain, right?" Lauren made a face that only threw gasoline on the simmering fire in Shawn's stomach.

"Hunter sent you a picture?" he asked. "When?"

"I don't know."

"Let me see your phone."

Her eyes narrowed. "Why do you care?" She pulled out her device and started scrolling on it.

"I just do."

"Wednesday night," she said, turning the phone toward him. "You two look so cozy together."

Shawn stared at the image of him and Lissa as they walked down the streets of the food and wine festival, their hands intertwined, and her dogs with them.

Lauren scoffed as she turned the phone toward herself again. "I don't care about her, Shawn." She put both hands on his chest. "We're good together while you're here in Miami. And when you're not...I have Seth."

Shawn wasn't going to split his life like that. Didn't even want to. "Hunter was on the island on Wednesday," he mused. "Did your father know?"

"Of course," Lauren said. "He sent Hunter the moment you called and said the Heartwoods wouldn't be selling." She backed up a couple of steps. "I don't even think you're listening to me."

Shawn's brain whirred as he realized several things. Jason didn't trust him. Hunter had been spying on him.

He hated both of those things, and he didn't want to be here.

"I have to go," he said, telling her the same thing he'd told Hunter. "Let yourself out."

"Shawn."

"Lauren," he said. "We're over. I'm not interested in anything you said." He glared at her. "Just go."

Her eyes filled with anger, and she grabbed her purse from his kitchen counter and stalked toward the door. He didn't care. He wasn't going to be working for her father much longer, nor was he going to be in Miami.

He emptied his suitcase by dumping the entire contents of it on his bed. "Call Alissa Heartwood," he told his phone as he started putting in shorts and T-shirts, sunscreen and sandals. Beachwear. Vacation items.

And still, Lissa didn't answer her blasted phone.

13

———

Alissa ignored Shawn's third call, just like she had the other two. Her father had returned from his fishing trip that morning, and the family was currently sitting together in the small living room at her parents' house.

It didn't matter what Shawn said anyway. His company was a joke. Dishonest. Ruthless. He'd probably been sent here to keep *her* busy while they got a land deal approved under the table, and the thought tasted like poison in the back of her mouth.

"Okay." Her father hung up the phone and looked at Olympia. "Our land is still ours. The Saddlers still have their land. The high-rise can't continue without one of us selling, and I've got Sergeant Myers pulling the video from the bank across the street from the construction site. We'll see who went in."

"What if they used the other side?" Alissa asked.

"There's only one way down either side," he dad said, sitting heavily on the couch next to his wife. "The camera is a wide angle. We'll be able to see them."

"John said the land was in the process of being rezoned," Olympia said. "Not true?" Her contact at the county offices had called that morning while Alissa was in her office, telling her about the vandalism on the high-rise. Things had exploded from there, and Olympia had called a family meeting.

She and their father had been on the phone for hours now, and Alissa felt sicker to her stomach with every passing moment. She couldn't image life on Carter's Cove without The Heartwood Inn. The miles of beach they had. The private cove where only she and *Big Blue* could go.

"Not true," he said. "We have to be publicly notified of that, and nothing has been filed."

"Why would he say that then?"

"Dominic Saddler said he did get notified of a filing of a rezoning request. We didn't. maybe John just assumed we both had?" Their father shrugged, but it didn't make Alissa feel any better.

"What about the heart?" she asked. "What did Dominic say about that?"

"Exactly what I did. He thinks the real estate developer is the vandal. Painted that to put suspicion on us, and we'd fight things out with the Saddlers." He sighed and leaned his head back.

The real estate developer is the vandal.

Alissa couldn't even swallow. Shawn would never do that to her. To her family. Would he? He hadn't even brought up the land deal again after they'd talked about it and he'd said he'd known they wouldn't sell.

That was the end of the story.

He'd been fixing up his motorcycle and spending time with her.

"Have you heard from him?" Olympia asked. "I know he's your boyfriend. Maybe—"

"He's not my boyfriend," Alissa growled, looking around. Not a single person in her family believed her. "Fine, maybe he was my boyfriend by mistake. But it was just a mistake. I don't really feel anything for him."

Oh, she was not a good liar. She didn't care what they thought. "He was just a boyfriend by mistake, I swear."

Olympia finally nodded, though she clearly didn't believe Alissa. They did have an understanding about falling for the wrong men, though. "Have you heard from him? Can you call him and see what you can find out?"

"It doesn't matter," her dad said. "We'll have that video in an hour or so, and then we'll know who did this. Dominic and I are willing to wait."

"I don't want to wait, Dad," Olympia said. "And *I* run the Heartwood empire now." She nodded to Alissa. "Call him."

She stood up, pure fear filling her from the soles of her feet to the top of her head. "All right. I'll be right back."

She got up and went out onto the front porch, surprised her sister didn't come with her. After all, Olympia didn't really care about privacy when she wanted answers.

Shawn's phone rang once before he said, "Liss. There you are."

"Hey," she said, wishing his voice didn't make her insides quite so soft. "We've got a real problem here. My family thinks you vandalized that building and made it look like we did. You painted a heart on the back door? Classy, Shawn."

"Wait a second." He pulled in an audible breath. "You think *I* spray painted that building?"

"Yes," she said.

"How could you think I'd do that?"

She didn't really, but the other seven people in the house did. "Just tell me you did it. We're pulling video footage from the bank across the street. It's over, Shawn."

"I did not do it," he said. "And I'm—I can't—I'll be back on the island as soon as I get a flight." The call ended without a good-bye, and Alissa stared out over the sandy dunes that led down to the beach. She had no idea what to think.

Back in the house, she held up her phone and said, "He's adamant he didn't do it. He's on his way back here."

"So we wait," Olympia said.

It felt like a week before her father's phone rang again, and he looked asleep. He jumped right up to answer it though, striding into the kitchen with the words, "Tell me you have it...Good...good. We'll be right over." He turned back to the family. "They have the tape. O, let's go."

Alissa stood up. "I want to come too."

"No," Olympia said. "I'll text you."

"O." Alissa stood right in front of her, her eyes searching her sister's. "It can't be Shawn."

"I hope it's not," she said. She hugged Alissa quickly and followed their father out the front door.

"Lissa—" her mother started.

Alissa held up one hand and made for the back door. She wanted to follow her father and sister to wherever they were going. But she also just needed to be alone. Olympia would text the moment she knew anything.

She headed down the beach to the cottage, where she collected her dogs and the keys to *Big Blue*. She wasn't going to go out into the cove, though. She just loaded everyone up on the boat and let the waves coming ashore rock her while she tried to reason through things.

There was no reasoning with her heart though, and it continued to beat out soft things for Shawn. Alissa knew he was more than a mistake, but she didn't know what to do about anything else.

She'd accused him of something terrible, and she wished she'd waited to see the tape. He'd sounded so hurt. If it wasn't him, had she just ruined any chance of getting back together with him?

"You're so stupid," she muttered to herself. "He doesn't even live here." Miami was two hours away by plane. She didn't want a long-distance relationship, and she flipped her phone over to send him a message.

Would you consider moving here permanently?

No way she could send it, but it was something they needed to talk about. They hadn't talked about hardly anything serious, as they'd agreed to a no-strings-attached couple of weeks. A sigh filled her whole soul—and then a message came in.

An image from Olympia, but it wasn't loaded all the way. The text with it came first—*Do you know who this is?*

Finally, the image loaded, and it was mostly black with some yellow-green light showing a man's face. He wore a suit, which was strange enough in the summer on an island destination, and he seemed intent on something in front of him.

His face was hard to make out, but Alissa pinched and pulled to make the image bigger. "That's not Shawn," she said, noting the softness in the man's jaw. His hair was also too short, and Alissa hurried to tap out a message back to her sister.

That's not Shawn. I don't know who it is.

Taking a chance that Shawn hadn't chartered a private jet out of Miami, she hurried to forward him the picture, with the same caption from Olympia.

Do you know who this is?

He didn't answer, and the notification that he'd read the text didn't come up.

Hours passed and dusk started to settle, and he still hadn't answered. The police had not found a single person on the island who could identify the grainy image of the man in the picture. The search felt hopeless, but at least the two families that had looked like they might go to war that morning had been pacified.

Alissa sat at her kitchen table, a bowl of cereal in front of her while her dogs begged at her feet. She'd eat and go to bed, because tourists didn't care what was happening in her personal life. They still wanted fresh fish in their restaurants, and it was Alissa's job to make sure The Heartwood Inn had the very best for its customers.

It was still early when she finished her pathetic dinner, but three o'clock in the morning came quickly. She'd just set her bowl in the sink when someone banged on her door.

A yelp flew from her mouth as both Dodger and Pirate began to bark and bark. They trotted over to the front door as if Alissa didn't know where the sound had originated from. They looked at her like, *Well? Come on! Someone's here!*

Alissa approached the door slowly, only giving whoever was there time to knock again. This time, a voice said, "Lissa. Open the door. It's Shawn."

Surprised, relieved, and angry, she flew to open the

door now. "Shawn." She kept a tight grip on the knob so she wouldn't take a swing at him.

He held up his phone with the image she'd sent him. "That's Hunter Reynard. He works at my firm."

"So he *is* with you."

Shawn's already dark expression stormed. "He is *not* with me. He has nothing to do with me. We simply work at the same firm. But thanks for the support. The vote of confidence. I can't believe you think I could do something like this to you or your family."

"Is that why you came back? To yell at me?"

"No," he said, much calmer now than before. "I came back to make sure this doesn't blow back on you or me." He held out his palm. "And I came for my motorcycle key."

Alissa's eyes widened. "I was going to work on the bike while you were gone."

"Well, I'm not gone anymore, am I?" His blue eyes blazed with furious flames. "Give me the key, Lissa. Bo said you came and got it."

She stood still for another moment, so many things running through her that she couldn't make sense of them. "Fine," she said, stepping over to the mantle where she'd put the key. "Here."

"Thank you." He turned to walk down the steps.

He was going to leave? Alissa's heart shriveled in her chest. This was not the reunion she'd imagined.

"So that's it?" she called after him.

"Yes," he said as he went down the stairs to the sidewalk. "Good-bye, Alissa." The use of her full name hit her squarely in the chest, and she almost sank to her knees. But Shawn Newman had broken her once, and she would not allow him to do so again. At least not in public.

She closed the door before she started to cry.

14

Shawn spent most of the next day in the hotel room he'd managed to find. It wasn't a great place, and it had cost twice as much as it should've. But they had space for a couple of nights, and he didn't want to spend another hour on Bo's couch.

Then he'd have to answer questions and talk about why he wasn't sleeping on the couch anymore. He didn't want to do either of those things.

Near mid-afternoon, he called Jason, knowing it would be a terrible conversation. The man didn't answer, which only proved to Shawn that he'd known all along that Hunter was behind the vandalism. That Jason had sent Hunter to Carter's Cove much earlier than he'd said he had. Everything Shawn didn't want to believe was true.

Not only that, but Lissa had suspected him. She didn't trust him, and that had cut the deepest. Stung the most.

"It's fine," he told himself as he hung up and then immediately dialed Jason again. Once more, the call went to voicemail. He said, "Jason, it's Shawn. I know you got the picture of Hunter entering that building. I don't know what game you two were playing, but I'm not interested. I'm quitting. Consider this my two-week notice, and my last day will be the last day of the two-week vacation I was supposed to have."

He drew in a deep breath. He had always enjoyed working for Jason. He hadn't suspected the man was capable of vandalizing his own building just to get two families fighting. What had he hoped to accomplish? That one of them would go bankrupt fighting in court, and need to sell their land?

Yes, that was probably exactly what Jason had been counting on.

"Good-bye, Jason." Shawn hung up, glad he hadn't allowed himself to get too emotional on the phone. He didn't need to go back to his office. He probably had some jackets there. Some ties stashed in a closet. A plant his secretary had given him for his birthday. Nothing important.

He would need to call his real estate agent to get his apartment on the market, and he'd definitely need somewhere better to stay in Carter's Cove than this dive of a hotel room.

Leaving the room, he started walking toward the epicenter of the island. The population of Carter's Cove was twenty thousand in the off-season, with that number doubling in the summer. It was a beautiful place to visit and live, and the tourism bureau had been doing campaigns to get people to the island at all times of the year.

He couldn't walk the whole thing, but the best beaches were on the south and east side of the island, with The Heartwood Inn right in the southeast corner—prime location for the best beaches and best views and best of everything.

At the height of tourist season, there was always something going on, and today's activities included a barbecue on the beach, with a movie being shown afterward. He finally hailed a pedicab to take him the rest of the way to the beach, and he joined in with the other visitors and families that had gathered for hot dogs, hamburgers, and potato salad.

A pang of sadness hit him. He used to love coming to these types of activities when he was a kid, and then a teenager. He wanted to be there with Lissa, but he had no idea how he could trust her again.

She obviously didn't trust him.

"Shawn Newman?"

He turned toward the male voice to find a guy standing there who looked somewhat familiar. Well, he would've been familiar twenty years ago.

"Bruce Thacker," he said with a smile. "I haven't seen you on the island in a long time."

"Yeah."

Shawn smiled and shook Bruce's hand. They'd been friends in high school, good enough to go to prom in the same group and hang out after football games. "I'm just back in town."

"To stay?" Bruce asked, and Shawn put a smile on his face.

"We'll see."

"Is your family here?" He glanced around as if Shawn's beautiful wife would appear from the sand.

"Oh, I'm not—I'm alone."

"Come sit by my family then," Bruce said, gesturing for Shawn to follow him. He didn't have anyone else to spend his time with, so he followed Bruce to a blanket where a woman and three children already sat.

"You remember Parvati," he said. "Parv, it's Shawn Newman."

She looked up at him, her dark eyes brimming with recognition. "Wow, Shawn Newman." She stood and hugged him. "What are you doing back in town?"

"Just...here," he said, taking up a corner of the blanket that wasn't already covered with napkins and hot dog trays. Bruce introduced him to all the kids, and they went back to their card games, chattering about colors and fish while they ate chips and drank sodas.

Shawn ate his hamburger and watched as the night started to take over the day.

"I saw you with Alissa Heartwood at the dog show," Parvati said. "Are you two back together?"

A gash opened up on Shawn's still-beating heart. "No," he said, throwing in a smile. "We're not together."

"Too bad," Parvati said. "I always thought you two were a cute couple, and she hasn't been out with anyone good in a while."

Shawn didn't know how to answer that, and thankfully, the movie started. Parvati didn't say anything else, and Shawn was left to his own thoughts about Lissa. They didn't take him anywhere good, and he ended up leaving the movie about halfway through with a promise to call Bruce if he needed anything.

But what he needed, no one could provide with just a simple phone call.

THE NEXT MORNING, HE DIDN'T LOITER IN HIS HOTEL ROOM. He had two more nights in the room, which meant he needed to find a more permanent place to stay. And a job. His savings would get him through a few months on Carter's Cove, but it wouldn't support him indefinitely.

So his first stop was Belle Billings's office, and the woman herself rose from the desk just inside the door.

"Well, I'll be," she drawled in her South Carolina accent. "It's Shawn Newman, back from the dead." She laughed as she crossed the room to hug him. "What are you doin' back here?"

"I want to move back here," he said with a smile. "And I've heard you're the best on the island, Belle." He looked around the tiny real estate office, noting how different it was than the office and building he'd worked in for a decade now.

"Oh, I am," she said. "Sit down, sit down. Your father didn't say a word about you comin' today."

"He doesn't know I'm here yet." Shawn hadn't told anyone in his family about his plans to relocate to Carter's Cove, and he supposed he should.

His phone chimed, and he glanced at it to see Lissa's name there. Instant fury lit up his mind as he sat down. "I'm keeping it a surprise for now," he said.

"Tell me what you want," she said, tapping on her keyboard and getting her hands in position. "And your budget. I'm sure you know it's not very cheap to live here, but we have some great properties. Renting or buying?"

"Whatever I can right now," he said. "Doesn't have to be big. It's just me. I do have a dog, and it would be great if there was a yard or a beach or a park nearby for him." Bo had not been happy about Gentleman being left at his house, and Shawn needed to go get the dog and get him some exercise that afternoon.

"One bedroom," Belle said as she tapped. "One bathroom. Yard. Park. Air conditioning?" She raised her eyebrows at the last one.

"Definitely," Shawn said. He'd work anywhere to be able to afford air conditioning.

"I have a cute little house on the north side," she said. "It's a rental at ten-fifty a month. I have two others in apartment complexes…I don't think you want those." She scrolled down the screen, her eyes squinting as she scanned. "And there's a house that just came up on Friday. Two-ten."

"When can we go look?" he asked. "I should've mentioned I'm in a bit of a housing bind."

"At your parent's house?" she asked with a knowing smile.

"Try at White Knight's," he said, faking a shudder, though the hotel definitely warranted one.

The smile slipped from Belle's face, and she reached for her phone. "Let me make some calls. No one can survive at White Knight's for long."

THAT EVENING, SHAWN WALKED INTO REDFIN, THE ON-SITE restaurant at The Heartwood Inn. He caught sight of Gwen, Lissa's younger sister, but she either didn't see him or didn't recognize him. He didn't care. He just wanted something good to eat to celebrate the great day he'd had.

"Just one?" the hostess asked, and he nodded.

"Yep," he said. "Just one." He followed her to a tiny table next to a window that looked out over the beach. He sighed as he ordered a soda and then let his eyes drift around to the other people in the restaurant.

He'd rented the house on the north side of the beach, mostly because it was completely remodeled and out of the way, exactly what he was looking for. He could also move in tomorrow, and that beat waiting to hear on a loan and trying to find somewhere to stay while he closed on a house.

Not only that, he'd asked Belle about the little corner shop next to the flower shop and if it was available to rent. She'd put him in touch with the owner of the building, and Shawn had a meeting with the man in the morning.

Lissa wanted that shop more than anything. At least in her dreams she did. Shawn needed a job, and he'd thought through all of his skills and hobbies, searching for something he could use the retail space for. He hadn't come up with anything yet, and he'd need to start job hunting the next day too.

But for tonight, he was going to enjoy fresh fish caught on *Big Blue*, and watch the waves come ashore until he couldn't see them anymore—and try to find a way to forgive Lissa.

If he could do that, maybe he could get her back in his life.

As he'd gone around with Belle today, signed paperwork, and made himself a permanent resident on the island, he'd found he'd wanted to tell one person—Lissa.

Sure, he'd called his mom and told her, and she was

excited. Bo was glad he didn't have to give up his couch anymore, and that Gentleman would be gone soon.

But really, Shawn wanted to share the good, bad, and ugly in his life with Lissa.

She'd forgiven him for the whole Marcy incident. He had to find a way to forgive her for thinking he could vandalize a building and frame her family for it.

That sounded so much worse that a teenage break-up, and he simply didn't know how to move past the hurt feelings, resentment, and anger.

Yet, he told himself as his waitress appeared with his drink and asked, "Ready to order, Mister Newman?"

He looked at the woman, probably a decade younger than him. "Do I know you?"

She grinned and tucked her hair behind her ear. "No, sir. But my boss said you're one of our VIP guests. Just trying to make you comfortable."

He looked past her, but he didn't see anyone he knew. "Your boss?"

"Yes." She glanced over her shoulder too. "Miss Heartwood? She said to make sure you have everything you want."

He didn't know which Miss Heartwood that was, but he just nodded and asked, "Was the halibut caught this morning?"

15

On Monday night, Alissa sat in Olympia's office, because she didn't want to go home alone. She'd hung around the inn yesterday too, and she'd stayed out in the cove for an extra hour this morning, as it seemed like the tourist population swelled with each passing day. She wanted to make sure there were enough fish and shrimp for the kid's night at the restaurant.

That had put her behind in the bakery, but it didn't matter. She had no one to meet. Nowhere to go. She went home for a couple of hours while the sun shone and to get the dogs out of the house, and then she went back to the inn.

People came and went at the inn, and Alissa could sit and people watch while the time passed.

Olympia had seen her and gestured for her to come

down the hall to the office. "You should just go talk to Shawn," her sister said.

"I...don't know," she said. "You didn't hear him, O. He was really upset."

"So are you," she said as she sat on the couch with a big sigh. "I don't even have a mistake boyfriend, but if I did and something happened, I'd go talk to him."

"I can't just show up and talk to him."

"Why not?"

"For one, I don't know where he's staying."

Olympia scoffed like that was a problem easily solved. "So you send a few texts and find out."

In all honesty, Alissa could do that and know where Shawn was in a few minutes. Her heart pulsed too many times in a single beat, and thankfully, her sister couldn't see it. She collapsed on the couch and leaned back into the cushions.

"I'm not going to stalk him."

"Your loss," Olympia said. "And just so you know, I didn't believe you when you said he was a mistake. I know it was only a few days, but you've been so much happier this week than I've seen you in a while."

Alissa wanted to argue with her, but she couldn't. It would all be a lie anyway. It had been wonderful having someone to spend evenings with, a way to see all the island happenings in a new way, and a good reason to laugh in a way she hadn't in a while.

"Oh, no comeback," Olympia said.

"Just don't," Alissa said. "I'm just not sure what to do."

"Do? I just told you what to do."

"I'm going to go home." Alissa started to stand, but Olympia held up her hand.

"Let's get sodas and nachos sent over," she said. "We can eat here or go upstairs. I promise I won't say anything else about Shawn."

"With pork?"

"With pork." Olympia smiled at her, a knowing glint in her eyes. "I'll call the kitchen right now." She picked up her phone and started putting in the order. "For my penthouse, please," she added. "Two plates."

A long pause followed, and then she said, "Gwen?" Her eyes met Alissa's, and there was something going on down in the kitchen. "Really? What table?"

She scooted to the edge of the couch and held up her hand as if Alissa was going to leave now. Of course she wasn't. She needed to know what was so interesting that Olympia had that sparkle in her eyes again.

"Thanks, Gwen." She hung up and stood up, her face glowing. "Guess who's right around the corner, eating dinner at Redfin?"

"Who?" Alissa asked.

"Shawn. Newman."

"What?" Alissa felt like someone had jumped on her chest with both feet. She searched her sister's face, sure she was lying. "Why would he come here?"

"It's it obvious?" Olympia asked. "He's hoping to see

you."

"No." Alissa shook her head resolutely. "No way. I never once said I came to the restaurant for dinner."

"The point, little sister, is that he's here. *Here.*" Olympia grabbed both of Alissa's shoulders. "Which means, Liss, that he's not mad at you. Or the family. Or anything. Why else would he come here?"

"He likes fish?" Alissa guessed.

Olympia cocked her head to the side. "Does he like fish?"

"Yes. No. I don't know." That about summed up how Alissa felt about everything in the moment.

"Come on," Olympia said. "We have to go pick up our nachos."

"They can't bring them up to the penthouse?"

"Oh, they can," Olympia said. "I just said I'd come pick them up." She grinned at Alissa. "And Shawn's sitting at a table near the pick-up counter."

"Olympia," Alissa said. "I'm not ready to see him."

"When are you going to be ready?"

"I don't know. When I have something amazing to tell him. Or show him."

Olympia started for the door. "What would that be?"

"I don't know. That's just it, O. I can't think of some-thing that will get him to see me."

"Just you being you is what get him to see you."

"No," Alissa said. "You're wrong. Would you have done that with Hunter?"

Olympia expression stormed, and Alissa reached out and tucked her sister's hair behind her ear. "It's been three years, O."

"I'm fine."

"Who's the last man you went out with?"

"I took over the inn," Olympia said. "I don't have time to date. But you, little sister, do. Now, let's go get your guy back."

"Olympia," she protested, stumbling a little as she got towed toward the door. "No." In that moment, the motorcycle popped into her mind. "The bike."

"What?" her sister asked.

"The motorcycle, O," she said, hope and excitement filling her bit by bit. "I can fix up the motorcycle and that will get him to talk to me."

Her sister paused, one hand on the doorknob. "That's actually a good idea."

"I just need to text Bo," Alissa said.

"And we need the nachos," Olympia said. "And you can take a peek at Shawn. He's probably crying over his halibut."

Alissa scoffed. "I'm sure he's not crying. Or eating halibut." That was her favorite fish, not his.

"Gwen said he'd ordered the halibut," Olympia said, opening the door. Alissa couldn't help smiling as she followed her sister down the hall to Redfin, where Shawn did sit at a table near the window, a plate of fish and fries in front of him.

Alissa couldn't help staring at him while Olympia waited for the nachos, but when Shawn turned toward her as if he could feel Alissa's gaze, she ducked behind another person waiting for their to-go order.

ALISSA SANDED AND BUFFED OUT THE SCRATCHES AND DINGS in the gas tank of the motorcycle, determined to get it finished this week. Her eyes itched and she kept coughing every now and then. But she was going to get this bike cleaned up and ready for the parade.

Then she was going to figure out how to get Shawn to talk to her again. She hadn't texted or called him, because his farewell on Saturday had sounded very final. But Alissa was well-connected around the island, and she'd heard that Shawn was still in town. She didn't know where, and she didn't know what his plans were.

But the motorcycle was still at Bo's, and she'd enlisted the man to help her work on it while Shawn wasn't around. Bo had texted to say Shawn would be coming to get his dog on Wednesday sometime, but he wouldn't be at the house before then.

So while Alissa desperately needed a nap, she spent Tuesday afternoon and evening, and most of Wednesday with Gentleman and the motorcycle.

The gas tank gleamed with the metallic red paint she'd chosen, and most of the metal had been polished and cleaned up. The seat wasn't finished, but her fingers hurt, and she really didn't want to get caught until she was ready to talk to Shawn.

And she wasn't ready yet. The motorcycle parade was now just a week away, and she sure hoped he'd be able to forgive her by then. The police had arrested Hunter Reynard in Miami, and he'd admitted to the vandalism at the high-rise.

No more work had been done at the construction site, and rumors were circulating around the locals on the island that the project would be abandoned completely. Alissa wished she hadn't called him when Olympia had told her to.

She'd said so many things about him that weren't true, and he didn't even know it.

Gentleman barked, and she startled. She'd worked right past the alarm she'd set for herself so she could get out of the backyard before Shawn showed up.

The dog continued to bark, and Alissa needed to get out of there. She hurried out of the shed and got the door closed and locked, her heart pounding and pounding.

"Hey, boy," Shawn said just as Alissa ducked behind the shed where they'd first found the motorcycle. She pressed one hand over her mouth and one over her heartbeat, hoping he'd just take his dog and go.

He chuckled, and she could hear Gentleman panting too. "I missed you, bud," he said. "Have you been good for Uncle Bo? Have you?"

Just the sound of his voice made her miss the few days they'd had together. She wanted to do all the summer activities with him, kiss him at night, and have him come out on *Big Blue* with her.

He'd never done that, and she almost jumped out from her hiding spot. Shawn's voice faded, and she felt his presence leave the backyard. She slumped against the shed, thinking at least she hadn't been caught.

Her hands felt rough, and she went back into the shed to make sure everything was back where it should be and that the plastic covered the motorcycle, just in case Shawn came looking. Sure, he could take it off and see someone had been here working on the bike. But she didn't think he would.

Bo said he'd found a place and was moving in. He wouldn't tell her where it was, and Alissa didn't need to turn into a stalker to see Shawn. He went by Redfin every evening, according to Gwen.

Her sister had been texting her more than normal, everything about what Shawn ordered to what he wore, and Alissa wanted to know why he kept going back to Redfin. She wanted to know what he was going to do in Carter's Cove to make his living, and she wanted to know if he thought about her at all.

All the same things she'd once wondered about him before, when he'd chosen Marcy over her.

She realized now she should've fought for him back then. At least gone and talked to him instead of shutting herself into her bedroom and pretending like everything was okay.

Her phone rang, and she hurried to pull it out of her pocket so she could silence it.

"Mack," she said in a near-whisper. "Is the seat ready?"

"Yep," he said. "I can't get it out to the island until Monday, though."

"Monday?" The seat was all she needed to finish the motorcycle, and the parade was on Tuesday. A Monday delivery would work, but what if Shawn wouldn't take her back after that? They'd miss the parade.

"Can I come pick it up?" she asked.

"Sure," Mack said. "You know where I am."

"What time do you close?"

"Six."

Alissa wasn't entirely sure what time it was, and getting off the island was a challenge in the summer. But she had to try. "If I don't come today, I'll be there tomorrow," she said.

"Great. See ya, Liss."

Liss.

She hung up and looked at her phone to check the time. Almost three-thirty. It could take an hour to get off the island, and that was with a ferry ticket and no tourists. Determined to go first-thing tomorrow after stocking the bakery, Lissa left through Bo's back gate, where she'd left the bicycle she'd rented from him for the week.

16

Shawn exhaled heavily, looking around the house he'd rented. He'd gotten everything moved in, and the house stocked with groceries, and now he faced a weekend without Lissa. There were plenty of activities to keep him busy, and he didn't want to do a single one of them without her.

Gentleman had already claimed the couch, and Shawn wondered what he'd do with all of his furniture from his place in Miami.

Feeling reckless, he pulled out his phone and texted Marty, his real estate agent. *All the furnishings can go with the apartment.*

All of them?

I'll come clean out my clothes and a few things, he texted. *But I found a great cottage here, and it's furnished.*

Yes, some of his stuff was nicer—a lot nicer. But he

didn't care. It would cost a fortune to get the bigger items across on the ferry, and it would be extremely difficult with all the tourists coming over from the mainland.

The ferry ride took about thirty minutes, and there were plenty of beach towns up and down the coast of South Carolina. But there was nowhere like Carter's Cove island, and Shawn said, "Come on, Gent. Let's check out the back."

He went out the back door, where he had a stretch of grass before the sand started. A fence separated the two areas, and this beach wasn't nearly as commercial as the ones on the south and east side of the island. The rocks were bigger, and the swells of dunes a little rougher, and Gentleman seemed very interested in exploring them.

Shawn chuckled as the dog started sniffing around, and he sat on the bottom step as he watched Gentleman. He thought of Alissa, and what she'd think of this place, and if she could park *Big Blue* down at the beach.

He'd been thinking about her for days now, and it had taken every ounce of willpower he possessed to stay away from the bakery in the mornings. He'd wanted to go in the moment they opened and watch that door for Alissa for hours.

He hadn't. And he wanted a medal for it.

Gentleman barked at the same time the doorbell rang. Shawn gripped the railing and pulled himself up. "Who's here?" he asked the dog as he streaked past and ran through the back door. Probably one of the neighbors who'd noticed someone had moved in.

Shawn whistled as he crossed through the house and pulled open the door. The song died in his throat as he came face-to-face with Alissa.

"Liss." Her name hissed between his lips. She wore a pair of shorts that had to be illegal in length and a tight T-shirt that said Carter's Cove across the front of it. Her blonde hair had been pulled into a tight ponytail, and she lifted her sunglasses to the top of her head.

She pulled in a long breath, but she still said nothing. Behind her, on a trailer attached to her car, sat the motorcycle he'd found in Bo's shed. At least Shawn thought it was the same bike.

"What did you do?" he asked, a hint of teasing in his voice.

"I wondered if maybe you'd like to go for a ride," she said.

"With you?"

"Yes." Her blue eyes held only nerves. "Shawn, I don't know if you think you can give me another chance. But last week was literally one of the better weeks of my life, and it was because of you."

She swallowed and motioned toward the motorcycle. "So I snuck into Bo's shed and fixed up the bike. Our first date all those years ago was at the motorcycle parade, and I want to ride in it with you."

Shawn smiled, the gesture slow as it filled his whole face. "You fixed up the bike."

"I fixed up the bike." She clasped her hands together and pulled them apart. "I'm sorry for thinking you could've vandalized that property and blamed it on me or my family. I never really thought that, I swear. Things were so tense, and my dad—"

"Liss," he said, silencing her. "Slow down." He wanted to go back to the motorcycle parade. And the best week of her life.

She nodded, falling back a step. "Yeah. Right. Slowing down."

"You want to come in?" He stepped back. "I don't have a job, so I can't afford to air condition the whole island." He grinned at her, disliking the anxiety still thriving in her eyes.

She stepped into his house and glanced around. "This is a nice place."

He brushed his fingers across hers, unsurprised when she flinched away. "I think I can give you another chance."

She turned toward him, her eyes searching his. "Do you?"

Shawn shrugged, glad she'd relaxed a little bit. "As many as it takes, actually. I kinda like you, Lissa."

Her eyes crinkled as she smiled. "I like you too, Shawn," she said. "For real. Not by mistake."

"Oh, there was no mistake last time, either," he said,

slipping his arms around her. "I can't believe you fixed up that bike."

"I really want to ride it with you."

"I really want to kiss you."

"Do it, then." She closed her eyes, and Shawn bent down, his lips barely touching hers for a moment. Just a breath. "I'm sorry, Shawn," she whispered.

"I heard you the first time." He touched the tip of his nose to hers. "And I lied. I don't just like you Lissa. I'm falling in love with you." He kissed her then, stealing whatever response she might have to his declaration. By the way she kissed him back, Shawn got the feeling she was falling for him too.

He finally pulled away. His voice sounded a bit unused when he said, "So let's go for a ride."

"We just need the key," Lissa said, taking his face in her hands. "You're really not mad at me?"

"I was," Shawn admitted. "But that faded by Sunday afternoon, and then I just wanted to see you."

"Is that why you've been eating at Redfin?"

"I came once," he said, tilting his head. "How did you know?"

"Gwen told me," she said.

"I've wanted to come to the bakery every morning," he said.

"Come out on the boat tomorrow."

"Oh, I'll have to go to bed right now to manage that."

He chuckled, dipping his lips to trace them along her neck.

"So no motorcycle ride?" She gripped his shoulders, her voice breathless.

"Fine," he said. "We can go for a ride. I have the key around here somewhere." He stepped away from her, not wanting to leave the house at all. She bent down and patted Gentleman, a few kind words for him as Shawn went to retrieve the key from a drawer in the kitchen.

"Ready?"

She straightened, her eyes bright with hope. "Yeah. Come see what I did."

"How did you know how to fix it up?" he asked.

"I watched some videos," she said. "I mean, it's sandpaper and paint. I keep *Big Blue* afloat, and that takes some tools too." She flashed him a flirty look as she moved in front of him out the front door.

"I had to go all the way to Garden City for the seat," she said. "And the ferry was intense. I barely got on with my package it was so full."

"Well, it's the Fourth of July weekend," he said. "Fireworks tomorrow night, right?"

"And Monday," she said. "And again on the actual Fourth."

"Can we go together?" he asked, stepping over to the trailer and starting to undo the holds keeping the bike in place.

"To the fireworks?"

"Yes." He paused to look at her. "All of them. I love fireworks."

She smiled and nodded. "All right."

He rolled the motorcycle down onto the ground and handed Alissa a helmet. "What's going on tonight that we can do?"

"It's the gumbo competition."

"Oh, right." He buckled on his own helmet. "I really don't like gumbo."

"How very un-Southern of you," she teased.

"How about dinner somewhere?" he asked, thinking he should probably tell her about the shop he'd rented. But something told him to wait, and he said nothing.

"Sure," she said. "I know several of the food trucks came in yesterday. The return ferry was booked for *hours*."

Shawn threw his leg over the brand-new seat of the bike, stroking his fingers down the shiny gas tank, and marveling at the gleam of the handlebars. "This bike is amazing," he said. "You did an amazing job."

Lissa climbed on behind him, snuggling right into him as she wrapped her arms around him. He didn't wait for her to say anything. He punched the gas, and they went flying down the street, their laughter mingling as it floated on the air behind them.

SHAWN SPENT THE NEXT COUPLE OF DAYS WITH LISSA FROM well before the sun went up until it started to go down. He was exhausted, but the time with her was worth it.

"So balloon festival tomorrow morning," she said, skipping in front of him as they walked down Main Street. He'd parked the motorcycle at The Heartwood Inn, and they'd been down to the beach this afternoon. Now, they walked her dogs among all the shops and shoppers. And later, they were meeting his parents for dinner at the best surf and turf restaurant on the island.

"Yes," he said. "How do you manage that with the bakery? It starts early."

"At first light," she said. "So we'll go for an hour, and then I'll go into the bakery."

And he'd sit in the corner booth like he'd been doing for a couple of days now, sipping coffee and waiting for her to come out and join him on her break.

"And the motorcycle parade that night," she said.

"I haven't forgotten." He smiled at her as they approached the corner shop. "Look," he said, nodding toward it. "The for rent sign is gone."

"It is?" She let go of his hand and stepped over to the windows, taking Dodger with her. Pirate sat down, his tongue hanging out of his mouth like he'd had enough of this walking thing. Lissa turned back to him. "It is. I wonder who rented it and what they're going to do with it."

Shawn's throat suddenly felt so dry. He swallowed,

feeling very much like Pirate in this moment. Thirsty and tired and hot. "I did," he said, his voice sounding like a croaking frog.

Lissa turned toward him. "What? You did?"

"I rented it," he said. "I need a job here on the island, and I figured I could be, I don't know. A management company."

She half scoffed, half laughed. "You can't make any money doing that. The rent prices here are already sky-high."

"Yeah, probably," he said. "I do need a job though. I was thinking of using it for something. A photography studio or something."

"Do you know photography?"

"You say that with such...disbelief." He shook his head. "But no, I don't really know photography. I was thinking I could watch some videos."

She blinked, and Shawn burst into laughter. Lissa joined him, and he wrapped her in his arms and held her close while they sobered.

"I was thinking maybe you should use the space," he said, looking only at her. "For a fish-mongering shop."

"Shawn." Lissa pressed her lips together, her eyes brimming with emotion.

"Don't decide now," he said. "Come on, my parents will be ten minutes early, which means we're already late."

17

Alissa gazed up into the sky, the morning sun painful in her eyes. She shaded them as she watched the balloons go higher and higher. "They're so pretty," she said, marveling at how they expanded and expanded, finally lifting off the ground with nothing but hot air.

Shawn's arm around her still felt a little surreal, despite the last few days they'd spent together. She'd enjoyed every minute with him, though they still seemed to take jabs at one another from time to time.

His parents had seemed happy that he was back in town, and Alissa couldn't express how much happier she was. Olympia had been right, and Alissa had made of point of telling her sister that. Encouraging her to get a new boyfriend of her own.

"I can't," she'd said. "I have someone coming to rent the other penthouse, and it needs to be spruced up."

But even Olympia had taken a break this morning. It seemed like everyone had come out to watch the hot air balloons, and for once, Alissa didn't mind the crowds on Carter's Cove.

"Look, there's a smiley face," he said, pointing to a bright yellow balloon as it lifted off from the crowd.

She grinned at it, feeling a smile move through her entire being. They continued watching the balloons take off, the blowing and hissing sounds from the fire filling the air around them. Soon enough, the crowd started to break up, and Shawn asked, "Breakfast?"

"I have to go to the bakery, remember?" She tucked her hand in his so they wouldn't get separated among the press of people.

"I'll drop you off and go grab something," he said. "Bring it back."

Alissa didn't argue with him. He'd do it anyway, and she rather liked him doting on her. He maneuvered the motorcycle through the crowds and to The Heartwood Inn, which stood majestically at the end of Main Street, almost an iconic building on the island. She hurried inside, determined just to do the basic desserts that day.

With so much going on outside on the island, surely they wouldn't need cannoli or crème puffs.

The first time she took a tray of brownies out to the

bakery, she found Shawn in the booth, a couple of brown paper bags in front of him.

"Ham, egg, and cheese croissant," he said. "From Bobby's." He nudged her bag closer to her as she slid into the booth. "And I think I got a job."

"Oh, yeah? Doing what?"

"Deliveries," he said, his face shining with anticipation. "I mentioned to Bobby how hard it was to get around the island, and he said he'd been losing money because he can't get his deliveries out."

"Okay," Alissa said, unwrapping her sandwich. "Why doesn't he use a bike messenger the way everyone else does? Surely Bo can rent him a bicycle."

"The orders are too big for a bike," he said. "But not too big for a motorcycle."

"You're going to deliver for Bobby's," she said. How in the world could he even want to do that? He'd come from Miami—ritzy, glamorous Miami—as a real estate developer. The man probably made a ton of money, had black leather in his office, and a secretary outside the door.

He hadn't said anything about leaving his job there, and Alissa didn't want to be the one to bring it up.

"I'm going to deliver for Bobby's," he said. "And not only that, I'm going to have a friend of mine in the city build me an app. I'm going to deliver for anyone and everyone on Carter's Cove." He looked at her earnestly now. "I need you to help me with a name."

She unwrapped her sandwich, this conversation moving so fast. "A name for the app?"

"And the business," he said. "I've been texting Bo this morning, and he thinks it's a great idea. Said we can wrap it into his corporation. I mean, he's already doing transportation. This is sort of like that. Here's how it works...."

He went on to explain how people could order from somewhere—a restaurant like Bobby's or Redfin, the flower shop, the bakery, the drug store—and he'd go pick up what they'd ordered and take it to them.

"Like the pizza places have been doing for years," he said. "But I deliver anything."

"Wow," she said. "Sounds amazing."

"So I need a name for it."

Alissa took a bite of her sandwich, the cheese melting into the ham. "Carter's Cove Concierge," she said. "That might be too long."

"Yeah," he said. "It might be. And I'm not really a concierge. I'm not telling you where to eat or about the best thing to do on the island." He lifted his coffee cup to his lips. "What about something simple, like Delivered?"

"What about like Speedy Service?" she suggested.

Shawn considered what she'd said. "I'll keep thinking about it. I'm talking to my friend later this week."

"What's his name?"

"Isaac Devonshire. He builds websites and apps. Does a ton of computer science for small businesses. That type of thing."

Alissa had no idea how something like that would earn Shawn any money. But she didn't need to know. She didn't understand how developing real estate made people money either, but it did.

"Well, I better get back to work," she said, sliding out of the booth. She stepped over to him and kissed him, tasting the coffee on his lips. "Don't be late to pick me up, okay? We have to be in line for the parade by five."

"I know," he said. "Five. And you're going to wear those red shorts." He licked his lips. "Right?"

She grinned at him. "Right."

ALISSA LOOKED AT HERSELF IN THE MIRROR, THE WHITE TOP with all the blue stars on it the perfect complement to her red shorts. She was nothing if not patriotic, and while the actual Fourth of July wasn't until tomorrow, the motorcycle parade was filled with red, white, and blue.

She opened her front door at the same time Shawn pulled up on the motorcycle, and he looked devilishly handsome in a pair of navy blue shorts and a red polo shirt. He didn't get off the bike, but grinned at her as she walked toward him.

"Nice shorts," he said, kissing her when she arrived.

"Thanks." She climbed onto the bike behind him, balancing as she tightened the chin strap on her helmet. She wrapped her arms around him, a sense of safety moving through her along with the thrill at being able to touch him like this so easily.

As they rode to the line-up position and then down the streets with hundreds and hundreds of people waving American flags, Alissa couldn't help grinning from ear to ear.

And she knew now as she'd known all those years ago when she'd first ridden with him in this parade, that he owned a piece of her heart. A big piece. Maybe all of it.

The parade ended, and they bought hot dogs and ice cream on the street, finally making their way to the beach to watch the fireworks. As the show exploded overhead, Alissa snuggled into Shawn's side and whispered, "I love you."

His arm around her tightened, and he said, "I love you too."

Shawn paced along the front porch of Alissa's beach cottage. It was so dang early, and while he'd been out on *Big Blue* with her before, today was going to be different. He'd already been on board the boat to hide the diamond ring, and now he was just waiting for her to get up and come outside.

The clock on his phone ticked to three, and then past it. Still nothing from inside. He hadn't told her he was coming this morning, but he had an open invitation to join her on the boat anytime he could get himself out of bed that early.

With summer picking up, and more tourists coming to the island each day, his Smart Service delivery system was growing rapidly. He'd spent the better part of the last eleven months working with businesses to get them signed up, get their systems automated, get his staff trained.

The app worked well, and Shawn wasn't the only delivery guy. He'd joined forces with Bo, and they used mopeds and motorcycles to get the items people wanted and get them through the crowds in a short amount of time.

Everything was going well, and he had five delivery guys now. They worked from seven a.m. to eleven p.m., and the three o'clock call time for *Big Blue* had happened less and less.

Until this morning, and now Lissa was running late. Finally, Dodger barked, and Liss said, "What? Who's there?" as she opened the door.

"It's just me," Shawn said so she wouldn't be afraid of his presence on the porch.

"Hey, baby." She stretched up and kissed him. "Did you say you were coming this morning?"

"No, I just couldn't sleep." Not a lie, though his insomnia was all due to the words he needed to say to her.

Her two dogs swarmed him and Gentleman, who'd somehow come along for this crazy early morning boat ride. The five of them made their way down to *Big Blue*, and Lissa backed away from the dock.

Shawn joined her at the wheel, half a step behind her so she could lean back into his chest. His nerves kept him silent for another minute. Then another. Lissa worked the nets, pulling in a huge load of shrimp and then moving over to a school of fish her radar had found.

"I think we're good for the day," she finally said, reminding him that he hadn't come along just for fun.

"Liss," he said, drawing her attention.

"Yeah?"

He opened the drawer in the engine room where he'd stashed the ring and held up the black box. "I have something to ask you."

Her eyes widened, and she looked from the box to him and back a few times.

"I'm in love with you," he said. "I want to be your husband. I want you to be my wife. Will you marry me?"

Tears filled her eyes, and she pressed both hands over her heartbeat. "For all you deliver, that wasn't a very moving speech," she teased.

He grinned though he felt like maybe the boat would tip, dumping him into the cove with all the fish and shrimp she hadn't caught yet. "I don't know what else to say. We belong together."

He was tired of going home alone at night. Tired of waking up with an empty space beside him. He wanted her with him, morning, noon, and night.

"What are you thinking?" he asked.

"I'm thinking I'd like to see the ring."

Shawn fumbled the box in his haste to open it. "If you hate it, we can switch it out to something else." He rather liked the big stone set on the gold, several smaller diamonds framing it.

"Shawn," she said, peering into the box before looking up at him. "It's perfect. You're perfect. Of course I'll marry you." She took his face in both hands and kissed him, her lips trembling the slightest bit.

Shawn took out the ring and slid it on her finger, admiring the look of it there. "I love this island," he whispered into her hair.

"I'm so glad you came back to Carter's Cove," she said just before kissing him.

He was too, though he'd never anticipated his life would change so much from what was supposed to be a visit to his hometown. "I love you," he said.

"And I love you, Shawn."

SNEAK PEEK! THE HEARTWOOD INN
CHAPTER ONE

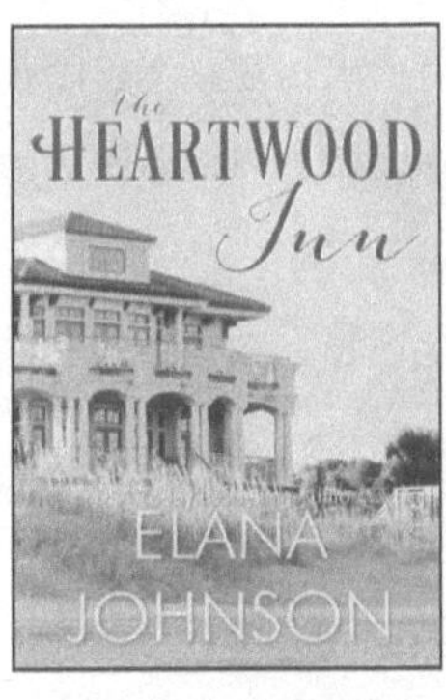

Olympia Heartwood wanted to throw her phone at the nearest wall. Then maybe it would stop ringing and dinging and notifying her of the zillions of problems around the inn.

Yes, she'd wanted this job. She was very good at dealing with problem clients and difficult employees. She'd been working in The Heartwood Inn since the age of ten, and as the oldest sister, the job had fallen to her if she wanted it.

And she wanted it.

She just also wanted a break every now and then. Maybe she'd like to eat lunch without abandoning her salad halfway through to go solve something happening on the outdoor patio.

By the time she got back to her office, the salad dressing had soaked the lettuce, and she could barely stomach salad when it was crisp. Soggy salad was worse than almost anything she could imagine, and she picked a candied pecan off the top and threw the rest in the trashcan.

"Sorry, Bianca," she muttered, knowing the woman who did housekeeping in this part of the inn would have to deal with the mess later.

Olympia sighed and pulled the folder of facts toward her. She'd asked her front desk manager to put together a list of things the new employees needed to be trained on. If there was anything she'd learned since taking over the inn last year, it was that there was a constantly revolving door of new employees.

And new employees needed to be trained.

The inn employed eight people at the front desk, as it was the height of summer travel, and the tourists streamed onto the island of Carter's Cove by the thousands. Their rooms at the inn had been booked for months, especially leading up to the surfing competition that South Carter's Beach sponsored every second week in July.

The check-in process was a bit slow right now, and she glanced up when her phone chimed. This one didn't have a special ringtone, which meant it was a family member or a non-essential person on her staff.

"They're all essential," she told herself as she saw

Celeste's name flash on the screen. Every sister had a job around the family business, and Celeste's was marketing, events, and the wedding planning service the inn provided.

Thankfully, her text wasn't about anything inn-related, but she wondered what she might wear on a date with her ex-boyfriend. Olympia picked up her phone, thinking of another ex-boyfriend that had recently come back into the Heartwood's lives.

Alissa had just started dating her high school boyfriend, and she and Shawn seemed to be very happy.

Do not go out with Andre again! she sent to Celeste, because while she was very good at keeping track of details and calendars and getting things ordered and delivered on time, with matters of the heart...Celeste needs some help.

It's not Andre, Celeste said. It's Boyd.

"Ew," Olympia said, though forty-year-olds didn't generally use the word. Even worse, she sent to her sister. *Why don't you go out with Benjamin? He was nice.*

Ben = Boring, Celeste sent back, and Olympia put her phone down. She'd love a man like Ben, who admittedly looked a little rough around the edges, what with the long hair and arms full of tattoos. He could make a surfboard obey his every whim, and while he spent plenty of time in the waves and perfecting his tan, he also had gainful employment.

Something Boyd did not.

He'd drain Celeste again, but Olympia didn't even twitch toward her phone. Let her sister figure things out.

Her phone pealed out the ringtone that indicated the front desk was calling. "Yes," she said, not phrasing it as a question.

"Miss Heartwood, there's a level ten guest on the line, inquiring about the penthouse on the twentieth floor."

"Put them through to me," she said. "Name?"

"Mister Chet Christopher."

She waited for the last name, but Nancy didn't continue. "That's it?" Olympia asked.

"Yes, ma'am. That's his whole name."

"Put him through." She always held back the penthouse on the top floor of the inn. Number one, there were only two penthouses in the building, and number two, she lived full-time in one of them.

To have someone on her floor with her felt...personal. Intimate. She'd have to share an elevator with them, and think about them up there with her. The pricetag was steep for the three-thousand-square-foot penthouse, and they usually only rented it out a few times a year, for large family gatherings.

The line beeped, and Olympia looked away from the training list in front of her. "Hello, Mister Christopher. I'm Olympia Heartwood. How can I help you?"

"I already told the other woman how I could be helped," he said, a slight accent to his words. A sexy,

Southern drawl that had Olympia sitting up though he wasn't in the room.

"The penthouse," she said. "Is only available for long-term rentals at the moment."

"That's what the website says," he said, a definite bite in his tone. "I'd like it for...."

His hesitation had her smiling. He thought he was so smart, and she realized all she had to do was quote an astronomical price or tell him whatever he said wasn't long enough. Case closed. Find somewhere else to stay.

"Well, for a couple of months at least," he said.

"Very well," she said, one of those cash registers from the eighties ringing in her ears. Cha-ching. "Our rate for the penthouse is monthly, and it's not inexpensive."

"How much?" Chet asked, his voice smooth now. So laid back. "I'm from the area, and I've been to Carter's Cove a few times."

Olympia could close her eyes and get lost in the tonalities of his deep voice. She snapped her eyes open, which had started to drift closed. "Five thousand per month," she said, sure he'd hang up on her.

"Okay," he said without hesitation. "When can I occupy it?"

"Tonight, sir," she said. "I can have the paperwork drawn up this afternoon." Giddiness pranced through her. Had she really just booked the penthouse for two months? Maybe someone was pranking her.

"That'd be great," he said, a measure of relief in his voice. "Can I check in by four?"

Olympia couldn't say no. That was the normal check-in time, but that penthouse would need to be dusted at the very least. She couldn't even remember the last time that room had been open, so the windows would need to be cracked too.

"Four would be great," she said, her voice as bright as the sun. "I'll let the front desk know you're coming."

"Thank you," Chet said.

"They'll have you come back to my office to sign the paperwork," she said. "And I'll take you up to the penthouse myself."

"Wow, a personal touch," he said. "That's great."

Olympia felt warm under the influence of his rolling, smooth, Southern voice. She leaned back in her chair, swiveling it toward the window and getting blinded by the bright summer sun.

"See you soon, Olympia," Chet said, and the line clicked.

Olympia set her phone down and then sprang out of her seat. She felt tied to her phone, but she used it to get Betty in housekeeping up to the south penthouse and to let Nancy at the front desk know about Chet Christopher and that he should be sent to Olympia when he arrived.

FOUR O'CLOCK CAME AND WENT, and Olympia felt buried beneath a dozen tasks that needed to be completed. She only knew what time it was because she'd set an alarm, and it had gone off twenty minutes ago.

She needed to go over the order for Redfin, the on-site restaurant that specialized in fresh fish and local cuisine. She didn't need to know the stock in the restaurant. She just needed to know how much it cost to replenish it.

She needed to know if housekeeping kept to their schedule, and if the guests were having a good time. She needed to know the pool got cleaned, and that the path to the private beach exclusive to The Heartwood Inn guests was clear, the towels stocked, the loungers in good repair.

The guests deserved the ultimate spa, resort, and beach experience, with a downhome touch. That was what The Heartwood Inn provided for families, couples, and anyone who came to the island looking for the best experiences of their vacation.

She worked through things systematically, her Paperwork Thursdays as long and boring as anything. But at least she only had to do this once a week—and the weekend sat right on the horizon.

Her desk phone beeped, and Nancy said, "Mister Christopher is here."

"Send him back," Olympia said. She stood and smoothed down her blouse. She carried about thirty extra pounds, and she knew she should get on the treadmill for just thirty minutes a day.

But she couldn't get up any earlier than she did, and she worked until she was so tired she collapsed into bed, fresh off the only elevator that led all the way to the twentieth floor.

She went to the door and opened it, stepping into the hall just as a tall man started to pass. Or maybe he was standing there. No matter what, Olympia ran right into him, getting the scent of the fabric softener he used in the dryer.

"Whoa," he said, that voice powerful enough to command horses and dogs—and apparently her. "Sorry about that. I wasn't sure which door it was, and well." He laughed, and that was so unfair. As were the pressure points of his hands where he'd gripped her by the shoulders.

"It's obviously this one." He grinned at her, and Olympia felt flushed from head to toe. She had to make sure he wasn't married.

Check for a ring, her mind screamed at her.

No, ask him.

No way she was asking him. Besides, he could lie, just like Hunter had.

"I'm sorry," she said, regaining some semblance of rational thought. She stepped away from his touch and smoothed down her blouse again. She suddenly panicked that she shouldn't have worn yellow. The color washed out her complexion and made her dirty blonde hair look even dirtier.

But she couldn't change now.

"Please come in." She gestured for him to enter, which he did. Olympia couldn't help the prancing nerves moving through her. This guy was extremely good-looking, and he'd be living across the hall from her for two months.

Maybe more.

"I have the contract here," she said. "We just need you to sign it."

"We?" he asked, glancing around at her office. "And did you know it took me ten minutes to check-in?"

"Some of our staff are new," she said, though Nancy wasn't one of them.

"Nancy said she'd been her for a few years." Chet looked at her then, and Olympia felt hot for an entirely different reason.

She cocked her head, sudden understanding washing through her. "Which hotel are you from?"

"I'm not from a hotel," he said.

"Right." She scoffed. "So you think I'm going to believe that you need a place to stay for two months, during the height of tourist season?"

"Your penthouse isn't occupied."

"And it's going to stay that way." Olympia folded her arms and glared. "I don't need a rival here, spying on everything we do at The Heartwood Inn." She couldn't believe she hadn't seen this coming from a mile away.

Stupid, she chastised herself.

Chet blinked. "I'm not a rival. I'm from Atlanta."

"There are plenty of hotels in Atlanta," Olympia said. "Bed and breakfasts. Inns. Vacation rentals. Resorts. Whatever you're calling it, it doesn't matter." She strode to the door. "Good day, Mister Christopher."

He stood there, surprise in his light green eyes, his brown hair all swept to the side like he'd just come off a movie set. He wore khaki shorts and a striped shirt, and she wondered for a moment how long it took him to shape his facial hair.

He didn't have much, and she had the sudden urge to run her fingers along his jaw and feel it. She made a fist with her hand instead.

"Good day?" he asked with a smile that had probably won over dozens of women. "Are we in England?"

That smile was not going to win over Olympia Heartwood, and she simply glared at him.

Read THE HEARTWOOD INN in paperback or ebook today.

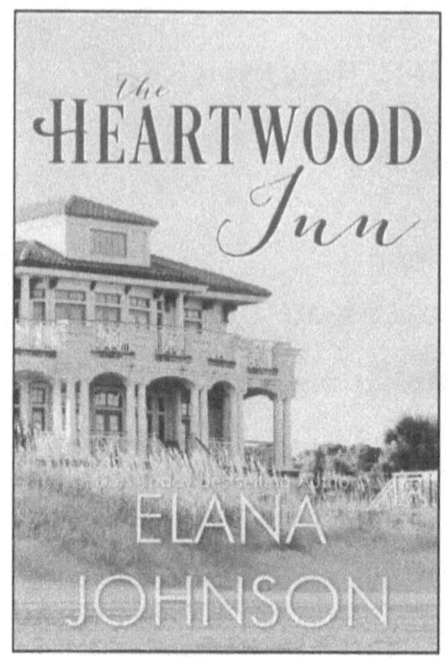

The Heartwood Inn (Book 2): She's excited to have a neighbor across the hall. He's got secrets he can never tell her. Will Olympia find a way to leave her past where it belongs so she can have a future with Chet?

The Heartwood Beach (Book 3): She's got a stalker. He's got a loud bark. Can Sheryl tame her bodyguard into a boyfriend?

The Heartwood Wedding (Book 4): He needs a reason not to go out with a journalist. She'd like a guaranteed date for the summer. They don't get along, so keeping Brad in the not-her-real-fiancé category should be easy for Celeste. Totally easy.

The Heartwood Chef (Book 5): They've been out before, and now they work in the same kitchen at The Heartwood Inn. Gwen isn't interested in getting anything filleted but fish, because Teagan's broken her heart before... Can Teagan and Gwen manage their professional relationship without letting feelings get in the way?

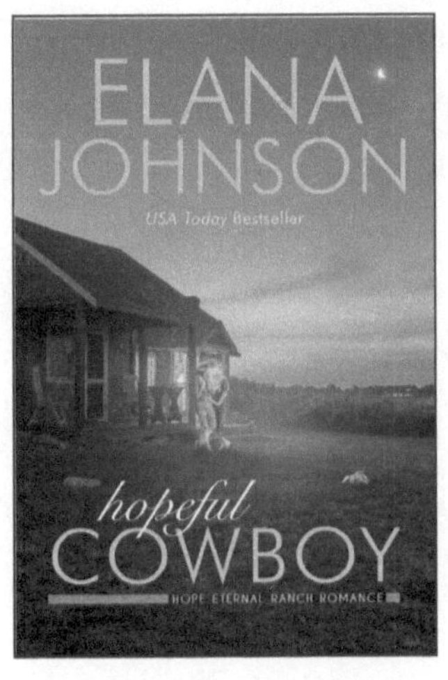

Hopeful Cowboy, Book 1: Can Ginger and Nate find their happily-ever-after, keep up their duties on the ranch, and build a family? Or will the risk be too great for them both?

Overprotective Cowboy, Book 2: Can Ted and Emma face their pasts so they can truly be ready to step into the future together? Or will everything between them fall apart once the truth comes out?

Rugged Cowboy, Book 3: He's a cowboy mechanic with two kids and an ex-wife on the run. She connects better to horses than humans. Can Dallas and Jess find their way to each other at Hope Eternal Ranch?

Christmas Cowboy, Book 4: He needs to start a new story for his life. She's dealing with a lot of family issues. This Christmas, can Slate and Jill find solace in each other at Hope Eternal Ranch?

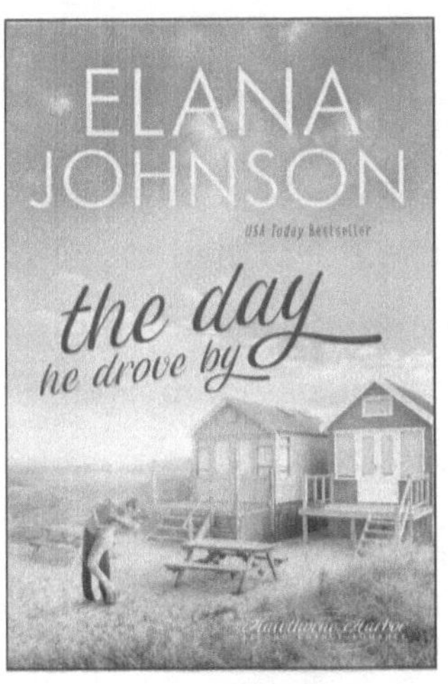

The Day He Drove By (Hawthorne Harbor Second Chance Romance, Book 1): A widowed florist, her ten-year-old daughter, and the paramedic who delivered the girl a decade earlier...

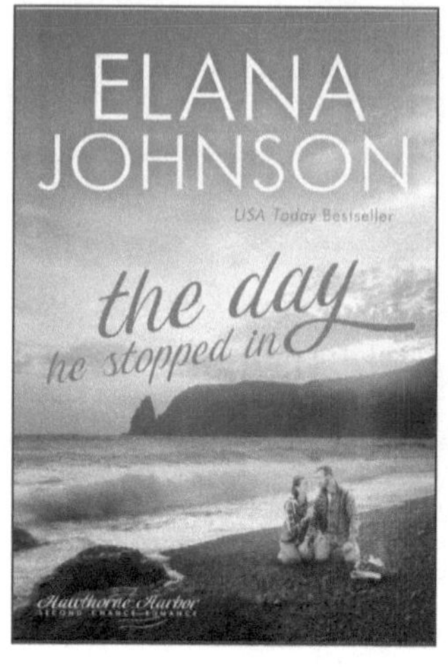

The Day He Stopped In (Hawthorne Harbor Second Chance Romance, Book 2): Janey Germaine is tired of entertaining tourists in Olympic National Park all day and trying to keep her twelve-year-old son occupied at night. When longtime friend and the Chief of Police, Adam Herrin, offers to take the boy on a ride-along one fall evening, Janey starts to see him in a different light. Do they have the courage to take their relationship out of the friend zone?

The Day He Said Hello (Hawthorne Harbor Second Chance Romance, Book 3): Bennett Patterson is content with his boring firefighting job and his big great dane...until he comes face-toface with his high school girlfriend, Jennie Zimmerman, who swore she'd never return to Hawthorne Harbor. Can they rekindle their old flame? Or will their opposite personalities keep them apart?

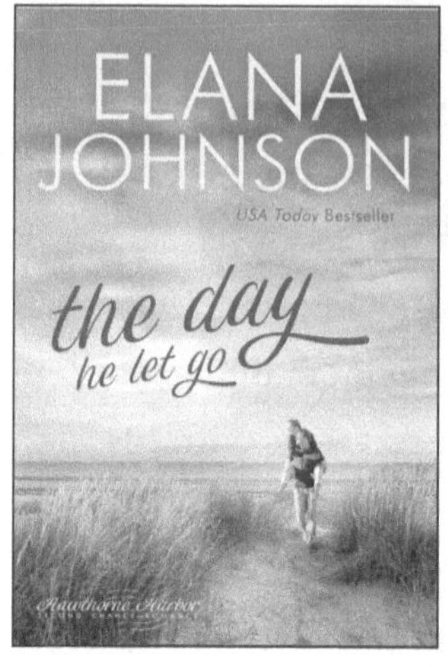

The Day He Let Go (Hawthorne Harbor Second Chance Romance, Book 4): Trent Baker is ready for another relationship, and he's hopeful he can find someone who wants him and to be a mother to his son. Lauren Michaels runs her own general contract company, and she's never thought she has a maternal bone in her body. But when she gets a second chance with the handsome K9 cop who blew her off when she first came to town, she can't say no... Can Trent and Lauren make their differences into strengths and build a family?

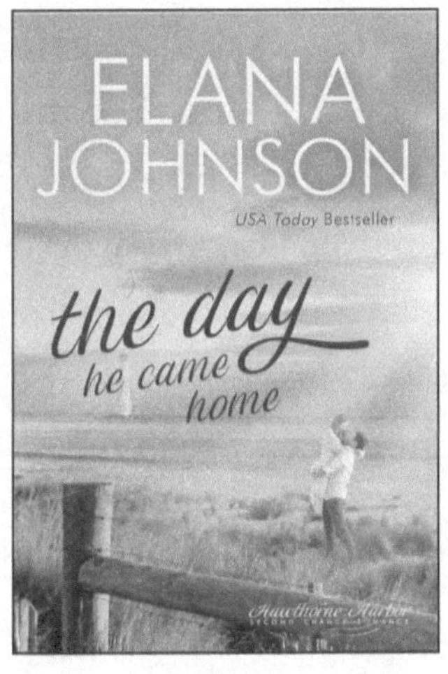

The Day He Came Home (Hawthorne Harbor Second Chance Romance, Book 5): A wounded Marine returns to Hawthorne Harbor years after the woman he was married to for exactly one week before she got an annulment...and then a baby nine months later. Can Hunter and Alice make a family out of past heartache?

The Day He Asked Again (Hawthorne Harbor Second Chance Romance, Book 6): A Coast Guard captain would rather spend his time on the sea...unless he's with the woman he's been crushing on for months. Can Brooklynn and Dave make their second chance stick?

The Billionaire's Enemy (Book 1): A local island B&B owner hates the swanky high-rise hotel down the beach...but not the billionaire who owns it. Can she deal with strange summer weather, tourists, and falling in love?

The Billionaire's Driver (Book 2): A car service owner who's been driving the billionaire pineapple plantation owner for years finally gives him a birthday gift that opens his eyes to see her, the woman who's literally been right in front of him all this time. Can he open his heart to the possibility of true love?

The Billionaire's Fake Engagement (Book 3): A former poker player turned beach bum billionaire needs a date to a hospital gala, so he asks the beach yoga instructor his dog can't seem to stay away from. At the event, they get "engaged" to deter her former boyfriend from pursuing her. Can he move his fake fiancée into a real relationship?

The Billionaire's Cinderella (Book 4): The owner of a beach-side drink stand has taken more bad advice from rich men than humanly possible, which requires her to take a second job cleaning the home of a billionaire and global diamond mine owner. Can she put aside her preconceptions about rich men and make a relationship with him work?

The Billionaire's Bodyguard (Book 5): Women can be rich too...and this female billionaire can usually take care of herself just fine, thank you very much. But she has no defense against her past...or the gorgeous man she hires to protect her from it. He's her bodyguard, not her boyfriend. Will she be able to keep those two B-words separate or will she take her second chance to get her tropical happily-ever-after?

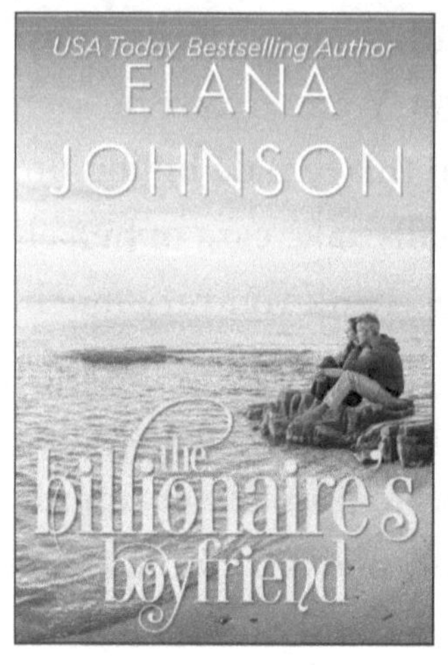

The Billionaire's Boyfriend (Book 6): Can a closet organizer fit herself into a single father's hectic life? Or will this female billionaire choose work over love...again?

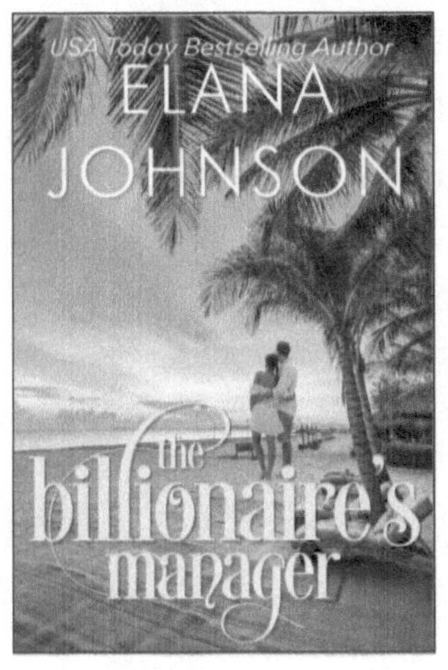

The Billionaire's Manager (Book 7): A billionaire who has a love affair with his job, his new bank manager, and how they bravely navigate the island of Getaway Bay...and their own ideas about each other.

The **Billionaire's Ex-Wife (Book 8):** A silver fox, a dating app, and the mistaken identity that brings this billionaire faceto-face with his ex-wife...

The Helicopter Pilot's Bride (Book 1): Charlotte Madsen's whole world came crashing down six months ago with the words, "I met someone else." Her marriage of eleven years dissolved, and she left one island on the east coast for the island of Getaway Bay. She was not expecting a tall, handsome man to be flat on his back under the kitchen sink when she arrives at the supposedly abandoned house. But former Air Force pilot, Dawson Dane, has a charming devil-may-care personality, and Charlotte could use some happiness in her life.

Can Charlotte navigate the healing process to find love again?

The Billionaire's Bride (Book 2): Two best friends, their hasty agreement, and the fake engagement that has the island of Getaway Bay in a tailspin...

The Prince's Bride (Book 3): She's a synchronized swimmer looking to make some extra cash. He's a prince in hiding. When they meet in the "empty" mansion she's supposed to be housesitting, sparks fly. Can Noah and Zara stop arguing long enough to realize their feelings for each other might be romantic?

The Doctor's Bride (Book 4): A doctor, a wedding planner, and a flat tire... Can Shannon and Jeremiah make a love connection when they work next door to each other?

The Rockstar's Bride (Book 5): Riley finds a watch and contacts the owner, only to learn he's the lead singer and guitarist for a hugely popular band. Evan is only on the island of Getaway Bay for a friend's wedding, but he's intrigued by the gorgeous woman who returns his watch. Can they make a relationship work when they're from two different worlds?

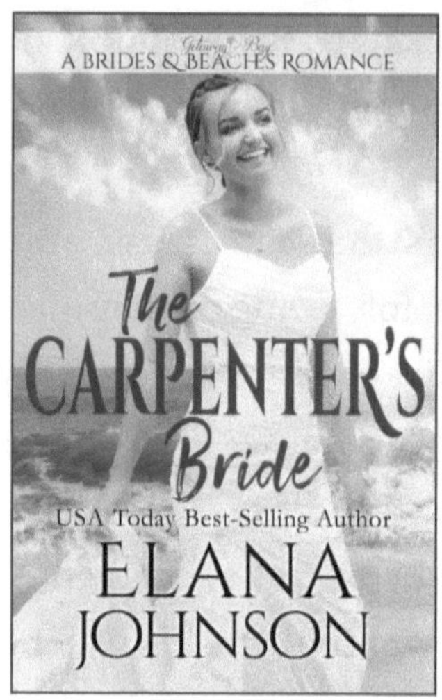

The Carpenter's Bride (Book 6): A wedding planner and the carpenter who's lost his wife... Can Lisa and Cal navigate the mishaps of a relationship in order to find themselves standing at the altar?

The Police Chief's Bride (Book 7): The Chief of Police and a woman with a restraining order against her... Can Wyatt and Deirdre try for their second chance at love? Or will their pasts keep them apart forever?

Love and Landslides (Book 1): A freak storm has her sliding down the mountain...right into the arms of her ex. As Eden and Holden spend time out in the wilds of Hawaii trying to survive, their old flame is rekindled. But with secrets and old feelings in the way, will Holden be able to take all the broken pieces of his life and put them back together in a way that makes sense? Or will he lose his heart and the reputation of his company because of a single landslide?

Kisses and Killer Whales (Book 2): Friends who ditch her. A pod of killer whales. A limping cruise ship. All reasons Iris finds herself stranded on an deserted island with the handsome Navy SEAL...

Storms and Sentiments (Book 3): He can throw a precision pass, but he's dead in the water in matters of the heart...

Crushes and Cowboys (Book 4): Tired of the dating scene, a cowboy billionaire puts up an Internet ad to find a woman to come out to a deserted island with him to see if they can make a love connection...

ABOUT ELANA

Elana Johnson is the USA Today bestselling author of dozens of clean and wholesome contemporary romance novels. She lives in Utah, where she mothers two fur babies, taxis her daughter to theater several times a week, and eats a lot of Ferrero Rocher while writing. Find her on her website at elanajohnson.com.